Sleep No More

P. D. James (1920–2014) was born in Oxford and educated at Cambridge High School for Girls. From 1949
to 1968 she worked in the National Health Service
and subsequently the Home Office, first in the Police
Department and later in the Criminal Policy Department. All that experience was used in her novels. She
was a Fellow of the Royal Society of Literature and
of the Royal Society of Arts and served as a Governor
of the BBC, a member of the Arts Council, where she
was Chairman of the Literary Advisory Panel, on the
Board of the British Council and as a magistrate in
Middlesex and London. She was an Honorary Bench-
er of the Honourable Society of the Inner Temple. She
won awards for crime writing in Britain, America,
Italy and Scandinavia, including the Mystery Writers
of America Grandmaster Award and the National Arts
Club Medal of Honor for Literature (US). She received
honorary degrees from seven British universities, was
awarded an OBE in 1983 and was created a life peer in
1991. In 1997 she was elected President of the Society of
Authors, stepping down from the post in August 2013.

Further praise for *Sleep No More*:

'When P. D. James died in 2014, readers lost a distinctive voice in crime writing. Her nostalgic style harks back to the golden age of the 1920s and 1930s, of Agatha Christie and Margery Allingham; James called on similar motifs from that era, but developed them further with psychological insight and gleeful darkness . . . The standout tale is 'The Murder of Santa Claus', featuring the classic closed circle set-up.' *Financial Times*

'The most grieved-for recent ghosts in the crime fiction library continue a consoling publishing afterlife with posthumous volumes of short stories: P. D. James with *Sleep No More: Six Murderous Tales*.' Mark Lawson, *Guardian* Best Crime and Thrillers 2017

'Extraordinarily clever, immensely entertaining and with a wintry theme that makes them perfect for the long dark nights ahead, these murderous tales are a dead cert for all crime lovers.' *Lancashire Evening Post*

'Unwholesome motive is at the heart of these six superior psychological tales by the late, great crime writer – perfect for fireside armchair reading. Rest assured that no crime goes unpunished by man or nature here.'
Kerry Fowler, Sainsbury's Christmas Book Club

the way . . . Wicked, sharp and often mercilessly witty crime stories.' *Thriller Books Journal*

'Each of these stories is a standalone story, all written in beautiful prose, full of twists, most of which you never see coming . . . I cannot recommend this collection highly enough.' *Nudge Books*

'This book offers a masterclass in the planning, plotting and execution of short stories that not only entertain and thrill but also explore the dark nature of humanity . . . *Sleep No More* packs a powerful punch. This is a perfect Christmas stocking filler for a crime fiction addict.' *Off The Shelf Books*

P. D. JAMES

Sleep No More

Six Murderous Tales

Foreword by
Peter Kemp

FABER & FABER

This edition first published in the UK in 2017
by Faber & Faber Ltd,
Bloomsbury House,
74–77 Great Russell Street,
London WC1B 3DA
This paperback edition first published in 2018

Printed in the UK by CPI Group (UK) Ltd, Croydon CR0 4YY

A CIP record for this book
is available from the British Library

ISBN 978–0–571–33988–4

2 4 6 8 10 9 7 5 3 1

Contents

Foreword

'Sleep no more' – the words that terrified Macbeth – strike horror into a house party in one of the stories collected in this book. They apply to characters in each of the others, as well. Anxiety-racked colluders in crime, unsettled witnesses of bygone killings, a murderer with bad dreams, and a troubled suppressor of homicidal memories populate these pages.

P. D. James's great accomplishment as a writer of crime fiction was to take the murder-mystery novel that had its heyday in the 'Golden Age' of the 1920s and 1930s and, by deepening it emotionally and complicating it morally and psychologically, give it a second golden age. In her short stories, she plays – half in tribute, half ironically – with the features that made the genre so addictively popular.

The narrator of the longest story, 'The Murder of Santa Claus', is a second-league writer of detective fiction who does 'a workmanlike job on the old conventions, for those who like their murders cosy'. Recalling a murder he had personal experience of when he was sixteen, he harks back to Christmas Eve 1939. In a Cotswold manor house owned by an unpleasant patriarch, an ill-assorted group assembles: a genteel couple on their uppers, a vamp in a tight evening gown, a severely efficient secretary, a famous aviator soon to join the RAF. Scarcely have the mince pies and punch been circulated before menace fatally mounts.

It's a classic scenario and, as with the title story of a previous P. D. James collection, *The Mistletoe Murder and Other Stories,* is placed within a wonderfully evocative resurrection of a wartime Christmas. An unsecured blackout curtain brings a reproving telephone call from an Air Raid Warden. On the wireless is P. G. Wodehouse's 'The Crime Wave at Blandings' (starring Gladys Young and Carleton Hobbs). The next day, the King's Christmas message quotes lines about a man standing at the gate of the year and asking for a light to guide him into the unknown.

The bombing raids and other carnage that unknown future brought are mentioned as the story closes, putting its teasing murder-riddle in perspective. Concluding twists in these tales don't only ingeniously confound readers' guesswork but sometimes redirect their sympathies. One ending contrives to be simultaneously poignant and sinister.

The prevailing tone is sardonically bracing. 'Mr Millcroft's Birthday', a very funny story about greed and snobbery getting their comeuppance, opens with a vigorously epitomising cameo: 'Mildred Millcroft, seated in the front left-hand seat of the Jaguar, thumped her copy of *The Times* into a manageable shape for reading the social pages.'

Sharp insights as well as corpses strew these stories. So do a hangman's noose, a blue poison bottle, a lino-knife, a revolver, a poker, sleeping pills and that fashionable toy of the 1930s, a yo-yo. Reading the use made of them, you share the pleasure of a writer gleefully and shrewdly revelling in the components of her craft.

Peter Kemp

The Yo-Yo

I found the yo-yo the day before Christmas Eve, in the way one does come across these long-forgotten relics of the past, while I was tidying up some of the unexamined papers which clutter my elderly life. It was my seventy-third birthday and I suppose I was overtaken by a fit of memento mori. Most of my affairs were tidied up years ago, but there is always a muddle somewhere. Mine was in six old box files on a top shelf of the wardrobe in my little-used spare bedroom, normally out of sight and out of mind. But now, for no particular reason, they intruded into my thoughts with an irritating persistence. Their contents ought to be sorted through and the papers either filed or destroyed. Henry and Margaret, my son and daughter-in-law, would expect to find that I, the most meticulous of fathers, had spared them even this minor inconvenience on my death. There was nothing else I needed to do. I was waiting, suitcase packed, for Margaret to come in the car to collect me for a family Christmas I would infinitely have preferred to spend alone in my Temple flat. To collect me. That is what we can so easily be made to feel at seventy-three; an object, not exactly precious but likely to be brittle, to be carefully collected, conscientiously cared for and as conscientiously returned. I was ready too early, as I always am. There were nearly two hours to be got through before the car arrived. Time to sort out the boxes.

The box files, bulging and one with the lid wrenched loose, were tied with thin cord. Undoing this and opening the first box, I was met by a half-forgotten, nostalgic smell of old papers. I carried the box to the bed, settled down and began leafing through a miscellany of papers from my prep-school days, old school reports – some of the inked comments yellowing, others as clear as if written yesterday – letters from my parents still in their fragile envelopes, with the foreign stamps torn away to give to school-friend collectors, one or two school exercise books with highly marked essays which I had probably kept to show my parents on their next furlough. Lifting one of these, I discovered the yo-yo. It was just as I remembered it, bright red, glossy, tactile and desirable. The string was neatly wound with only the looped end for the finger showing. My hand closed round the smooth wood. The yo-yo precisely fitted my palm. It felt cold to the touch, even to my hand which is now seldom warm. And with that touch the memories came flooding back. The verb is trite but accurate; they came like a full tide, sweeping me back to the same day sixty years ago, December 23rd 1936, the day of the murder.

I was at prep school in Surrey and was, as usual, to spend Christmas with my widowed grandmother in her small manor house in west Dorset. The rail journey was tedious, requiring two changes, and there was no local station, so she usually sent her own car and driver to collect me. But this year was different. The headmaster called me into his study to explain.

'I've had this morning a telephone call from your grandmother, Charlcourt. It appears that her chauffeur is unwell and will be unable to fetch you. I've arranged for Carter to drive you down to Dorset in my personal car. I need him until after lunch so it will be a later arrival than usual. Lady Charlcourt has kindly offered him a bed for the night. And Mr Michaelmass will be travelling with you. Lady Charlcourt has invited him to spend Christmas at the manor, but no doubt she has already written to you about that.'

She hadn't, but I didn't say so. My grandmother wasn't fond of children and tolerated me more from family feeling – I was, after all, like her only son, the necessary heir – than from any affection. She did her dutiful best each Christmas to see that I was kept reasonably happy and out of mischief. There was a sufficiency of toys appropriate to my sex and age, purchased by her chauffeur on written suggestions from my mother, but there was no laughter, no young companionship, no Christmas decorations and no emotional warmth. I suspected that she would much have preferred to spend Christmas alone than with a bored, restless and discontented child. I don't blame her. I have reached her age and I feel exactly the same.

But as I closed the door of the headmaster's study my heart was heavy with resentment and disgust. Didn't she know anything about me or the school? Didn't she realise that the holiday would be boring enough without the sharp eyes and sarcastic tongue of Mike the Menace? He was easily the most unpopular master in the school, pedantic, over-strict and given to that biting sarcasm which boys find more difficult to bear than shouted insults. I know now that he was a brilliant teacher. It was to Mike the Menace that I largely owe my public-school scholarship. Perhaps it was this knowledge and the fact that he had been at Balliol with my father which had prompted my grandmother's invitation. My father might even have written to suggest it. I was less surprised that Mr Michaelmass had accepted. The comfort and excellent food at the manor would be a welcome change from the spartan living and institutional cooking at school.

The journey was as boring as I had expected. When the elderly Hastings was at the wheel, he would let me sit in the front seat beside him and keep me happy with chat about my father's childhood; instead, I was closeted in the back with a silent Mr Michaelmass. The glass partition between us and the driver was closed and all I could see was the back of the rigid uniform hat, which the head-master always insisted that Carter should wear when acting as chauffeur, and his gloved hands on the wheel.

Carter wasn't really a chauffeur but was required to drive the headmaster when his prestige demanded this addition to his status. For the rest of the time Carter was part groundsman, part odd-job man. His wife, frail and gentle-faced and looking as young as a girl, was matron at one of the three boarding houses. His son, Timmy, was a pupil at the school. Only later did I fully understand this curious arrangement. Carter was what I had overheard one of the parents describe as 'a most superior type of man'. I never knew what personal mis-fortune had brought him to his job at the school. The headmaster got Carter's and his wife's services cheaply by offering them accommodation and free education for their son. He probably paid them a pittance. If Carter resented this, we, the boys, never knew. We got used to seeing him about the grounds, tall, white-faced, dark-haired, and, when not busy, playing always with the red yo-yo. It was a fashionable toy in the 1930s and Carter was adept at the spectacular throws which the rest of us practised with our own yo-yos but never achieved.

Timmy was an undersized, delicate, nervous child. He sat always at the back of the class, neglected and ignored. One of the boys, a more egregious snob than the rest of us, said, 'I don't see why we have to have that creep Timmy in class with us. That's not why my father pays the fees.' But the rest of us didn't mind one way or the other, and in Mike the Menace's class Timmy was a positive asset, diverting from the rest of us the terror of that sharp, sarcastic tongue. I don't think in Mr Michaelmass's case the cruelty had anything to do with snobbery, or even that he recognised his behaviour as cruel. He was simply unable to tolerate wasting his teaching skills on an unresponsive and unintelligent boy.

But none of this occupied my mind on the journey. Sitting well apart from Mr Michaelmass in the corner of the car, I was sunk in a reverie of resentment and despair. My companion preferred to be driven in darkness as well as silence, and we had no light. But I had brought with me a paperback and a slender torch and asked him if it would disturb him if I read. He replied, 'Read, by all means, boy,' and sank back into the collar of his heavy tweed coat.

I took out my copy of *Treasure Island* and tried to concentrate on the small moving pool of light. Hours passed. We were driven through small towns and villages, and it was a relief from boredom to look out at brightly lit streets, the decorated gaudy windows of the shops and the busy stream of late shoppers. In one village a little group of carol singers accompanied by a brass band were jangling their collecting boxes. The sound seemed to follow us as we left the brightness behind. We seemed to be travelling through a dark eternity. I was, of course, familiar with the route, but Hastings normally called for me in the morning of December 23rd so that we did most of the drive in daylight. Now, sitting beside that silent figure in the gloom of the car and with blackness pressing against the windows like a heavy blanket, the journey seemed interminable. Then I sensed that we were climbing, and soon I could hear the distant rhythmic thudding of the sea. We must be on the coast road. It would not be long now. I shone my torch on the face of my wristwatch. Half past five. We should be at the manor in less than an hour.

And then Carter slowed the car and bumped gently onto the grass verge. The car stopped. He pulled back the glass partition and said, 'I'm sorry, Sir. I need to get out. A call of nature.'

The euphemism made me want to giggle. Mr Michaelmass hesitated for a moment, then said, 'In that case we'd better all get out.'

Carter came round and punctiliously opened the door. We stepped out onto lumpy grass, and into black darkness and the swirl of snow. The sea was no longer a background murmur but a crashing tumult of sound. I was at first aware of nothing but the snowflakes on my cheeks, the two dark figures close to me, the utter blackness of the night and the keen salty tang of the sea. Then, as my eyes became accustomed to the darkness, I could see the shape of a huge rock to my left.

Mr Michaelmass said, 'Go behind that boulder, boy. Don't take long. And don't go wandering off.'

I stepped closer to the boulder, but not behind it, and the two figures moved out of sight, Mr Michaelmass walking straight ahead and Carter to the right. A minute later, turning from the rock face, I could see nothing, not the car or either of my companions. It would be wise to wait until one of them reappeared. I plunged my hand into my pocket and, almost without thinking, took out the torch and shone it over the headland. The beam of light was narrow but bright. And in that moment, instantaneously, I saw the act of murder.

Mr Michaelmass was standing very still about thirty yards away, a dark shape outlined against the lighter sky. Carter must have moved up silently behind him on the thin carpet of snow. Now, in that second when the dark figures were caught in the beam, I saw Carter violently lunge forward, arms outstretched, and seemed to feel in the small of my back the strength of that fatal push. Without a sound Mr Michaelmass disappeared from view. There had been two shadowy figures; now there was one.

Carter knew that I had seen; how could he help it? The beam of light had been too late to stop the action, but now he turned and it shone full on his face. We were alone together on the headland. Curiously I felt absolutely no fear. I suppose that what I did feel was surprise. We moved towards each other almost like automata. I said, hearing the note of simple wonder in my voice, 'You pushed him over. You murdered him.'

He said, 'I did it for the boy. God help me, I did it for Timmy. It was him or the boy.'

I stood for a moment silently regarding him, aware again of the soft liquid touch of the snow melting on my cheeks. I shone the torch down and saw that the two sets of footprints were already no more than faint smudges on the snow. Soon they would be obliterated under that white blanket. Then, still without speaking, I turned and we walked back to the car together, almost companionably, as if nothing had happened, as if that third person was walking by our side. I have a memory, but perhaps I may be wrong, that at one place Carter seemed to stumble and I held his arm to steady him. When we reached the car he said, his voice dull and without hope, 'What are you going to do?'

'Nothing. What is there to do? He slipped and fell over the cliff. We weren't there. We didn't see, either of us. You were with me at the time. We were both together by that rock. You never left my side.'

He said nothing for the moment, and when he did speak I had to strain my ears to hear.

'I planned it, God help me. I planned it, but it was fate. If it was meant to be, then it would be.'

The words meant little at the time, but later, when I was older, I think I understood what he was saying. It was one way, perhaps the necessary way, to absolve himself from responsibility. That push hadn't been the overwhelming impulse of the moment. He had planned the deed, had chosen the place and the time. He knew exactly what he meant to do. But so much had been outside his control. He couldn't be sure that Mr Michaelmass would want to leave the car, or that he would stand so conveniently close to the edge of the cliff. He couldn't be sure that the darkness would be so absolute or that I would stand sufficiently apart. And one thing had worked against him; he hadn't known about my torch. If the attempt had failed, would he have tried again? Who can know? It was one of the many questions I never asked him.

He opened the rear door for me, suddenly standing upright, a deferential chauffeur doing his job. As I got in I turned and said, 'We must stop at the first police station and let them know what has happened. Leave the talking to me. And we'd better say that it was Mr Michaelmass, not you, who wanted to stop the car.'

I look back now with some disgust at my childish arrogance. The words had the force of a command. If he resented it he made no sign. And he did leave the talking to me, merely quietly confirming my story. I told it first at the police station in the small Dorset town which we reached within fifteen minutes. Memory is always disjointed, episodic. Some impulse of the mind presses the button and, like a colour transparency, the picture is suddenly thrown on the screen, vivid, immobile, a glowing instant fixed in time between the long stretches of dark emptiness. At the police station I remember a tall lamp with the snowflakes swirling out of darkness to die like moths against the glass, a huge coal fire in a small office which smelt of furniture polish and coffee, a Sergeant, huge, imperturbable, taking down the details, the heavy oilskin capes of the policemen as they stamped out to begin the search. I had decided precisely what I would say.

'Mr Michaelmass told Carter to stop the car and we got out. He said it was a call of nature. Carter and I went to the left by a large boulder and Mr Michaelmass walked ahead. It was so dark we didn't see him after that. We both waited for him, I suppose for about five minutes, but he still didn't appear. Then I took out my torch and we explored. We could just see his footsteps to the edge of the cliff but they were getting very faint. We still hung around and called, but he didn't reappear, so we knew what had happened.'

The Sergeant said, 'Hear anything, did you?'

I was tempted to say, 'Well I did think I heard one sharp cry, but I thought it could be a bird,' but I resisted the temptation. Would there be a seagull flying in that darkness? Better to keep the story simple and stick to it.

I have sent a number of men down for life because they have neglected that simple rule.

The Sergeant said that he would organise a search, but that there was little chance of finding any trace of Mr Michaelmass that night. They would have to wait for first light. He added, 'And if he went over where I think he did, we may not retrieve the body for weeks.' He took the addresses of my grandmother and the school and let us go.

I have no clear memory of our arrival at the manor, perhaps because recollection is overshadowed by what happened next morning. Carter, of course, breakfasted with the servants while I was in the dining room with my grandmother. We were still in the middle of our toast and marmalade when the parlour-maid announced that the Chief Constable, Colonel Neville, had called. My grandmother asked that he be shown into the library, and left the dining room immediately. Less than a quarter of an hour later I was summoned.

And now my memory is sharp and clear, every word remembered as if it were yesterday. My grandmother was sitting in a high-backed leather chair before the fire. It had only recently been lit and the room struck me as chill. The wood was still crackling and the coals hadn't yet caught fire. There was a large desk set in the middle of the room where my grandfather used to work, and the Chief Constable was sitting behind it. In front of it stood Carter, rigid as a soldier called before his commanding officer. And on the desk, precisely placed in front of the Colonel, was the red yo-yo.

Carter turned briefly as I entered and gave me one single look. Our eyes held for no more than three seconds before he turned away but I saw in his eyes – how could I not? – that wild mixture of fear and pleading. I have seen it many times since from prisoners in the dock awaiting the pronouncement of my sentence, and I have never been able to encounter it with equanimity. Carter needn't have worried; I had relished too much the power of that first decision, the heady satisfaction of being in control, to think of betraying him now or ever. And how could I betray him? Wasn't I now his accomplice in guilt?

Colonel Neville was stern-faced. He said, 'I want you to listen to my questions very carefully and tell me the exact truth.'

My grandmother said, 'Charlcourts don't lie.'

'I know that, I know that.' He kept his eyes on me. 'Do you recognise this yo-yo?'

'I think so, Sir, if it's the same one.'

My grandmother broke in. 'It was found on the edge of the cliff where Mr Michaelmass fell. Carter says that it isn't his. Is it yours?'

She shouldn't have spoken, of course. And I wondered at the time why the Chief Constable should have allowed her to be present at the interview. Later I realised that he had had no choice. Even in those less child-centred times a juvenile would not have been questioned without a responsible adult present. The Colonel's frown of displeasure at the intervention was so brief that I almost missed it. But I didn't miss it. I was alive, gloriously alive, to every nuance, every gesture.

I said, 'Carter is telling the truth, Sir. It isn't his. It's mine. He gave it to me before we started out. While we were waiting for Mr Michaelmass.'

'Gave it to you? Why should he do that?' My grandmother's voice was sharp. I turned towards her.

'He said it was because I'd been kind to Timmy. Timmy is his son. The boys rag him rather.'

The Colonel's voice had changed. 'Was this yo-yo in your possession when Mr Michaelmass fell to his death?'

I looked him straight in the eyes. 'No, Sir. Mr Michaelmass confiscated it during the journey. He saw me fiddling with it and asked me how I came by it. I told him and he took it from me. He said, "Whatever the other boys may choose to do, a Charlcourt should know that pupils don't take presents from a servant."'

I had subconsciously mimicked Mr Michaelmass's dry sarcastic tone and the words came out with utterly convincing verisimilitude. But they probably would have believed me anyway. Why not? A Charlcourt doesn't lie.

The Colonel asked, 'And what did Mr Michaelmass do with the yo-yo when he'd confiscated it?'

'He put it in his coat pocket, Sir.'

The Chief Constable leant back in his chair and looked over at my grandmother. 'Well, that's plain enough. It's obvious what happened. He made some adjustments to his clothing . . .'

He paused, perhaps feeling some delicacy, but my grandmother was made of tougher metal. She said, 'Perfectly plain. He walked away from Carter and the boy not realising that he was dangerously close to the cliff edge. He took off his gloves to undo his flies and stuffed the gloves in his pockets. When he pulled them out again the yo-yo fell. He wouldn't hear it on the snow. Then, disorientated by the darkness, he took a step in the wrong direction, slipped and fell.'

Colonel Neville turned to Carter. 'It was a stupid place to stop, but you weren't to know that.'

Carter said, through lips almost as white as his face, 'Mr Michaelmass asked me to stop the car, Sir.'

'Of course, of course, I realise that. It wasn't your place to argue. You've made your statement. There's no reason for you to stay on here. You'd better get back to the school and your duties. You'll be needed for the inquest, but that probably won't be for some time. We haven't found the body yet. And pull yourself together, man. It wasn't your fault. I suppose by not saying at once that you'd given the yo-yo to the boy you were trying to protect him. It was quite unnecessary. You should have told the whole truth, just as it happened. Concealing facts always leads to trouble. Remember that in future.'

Carter said, 'Yes, Sir. Thank you, Sir,' turned quietly and left.

When the door had closed behind him, Colonel Neville got up from his chair and moved over to the fire, standing with his back to it, rocking gently on his heels and looking down at my grandmother. They seemed to have forgotten my presence. I moved over to the door and stood there quietly beside it, but I didn't leave.

The Chief Constable said, 'I didn't want to mention it while Carter was here, but you don't think there's any possibility that he jumped?'

My grandmother's voice was calm. 'A suicide? It did cross my mind. It was odd that he told the boy to go over to the boulder and he walked on into the darkness alone.'

The Colonel said, 'A natural wish for privacy, perhaps.'

'I suppose so.' She paused, then went on, 'He lost his wife and a child, you know. Soon after they married. Killed in a car crash. He was driving at the time. He never got over it. I don't think anything mattered to him after that, except perhaps his teaching. My son says that he was one of the most gifted men of his year at

Oxford. Everyone predicted a brilliant academic career for him. And what did he end up by doing? Stuck in a prep school wasting his talent on small boys. Perhaps he saw it as some kind of penance.'

The Colonel asked, 'No relations?'

'None, as far as I know.'

The Colonel continued, 'I won't raise the possibility of suicide at the inquest, of course. Unfair to his memory. And there isn't a shred of proof. Accidental death is far more likely. It will be a loss for the school, of course. Was he popular with the boys?'

My grandmother said, 'I shouldn't think so. Highly unlikely, I would have said. They're all barbarians at that age.'

I slipped out of the door, still unobserved.

I began to grow up during that Christmas week. I realised for the first time the insidious temptations of power, the exhilaration of feeling in control of people and events, the power of patronage. And I learnt another lesson, best expressed by Henry James. 'Never say you know the last word about any human heart.' Who would have believed that Mr Michaelmass had once been a devoted father, a loving husband? I like to believe that the knowledge made me a better lawyer, a more compassionate judge, but I'm not sure. The essential self is fixed well before the thirteenth birthday. It may be influenced by experience but it is seldom changed.

Carter and I never spoke about the murder again, not even when we attended the inquest together seven weeks later. Back at school we hardly saw each other; after all, I was a pupil, he a servant. I shared the snobbery of my caste. And what Carter and I shared was a secret, not a friendship, not a life. But I would occasionally watch him pacing the side of the rugger field, his hands twitching as if there was something he missed.

And did it answer? A moralist, I suppose, would expect us both to be racked with guilt and the new master to be worse than Mr Michaelmass. But he wasn't. The headmaster's wife was not without influence, and I can imagine her saying, 'He was a wonderful teacher, of course, but not really popular with the boys. Perhaps, dear, you could find someone a little gentler, and a man we don't have to feed during the holidays.'

So Mr Wainwright came, a nervous, newly qualified teacher. He didn't torment us – but we tormented him. A boys' prep school, after all, is a microcosm of the world outside. But he took trouble with Timmy, giving him special care, perhaps because Timmy was the only boy who didn't bully him. And Timmy blossomed under his loving patience.

And the murder answered in another way – or I suppose you could argue that it did. Three years later the war broke out and Carter joined up immediately. He was one of the most decorated Sergeants of the war, awarded the Victoria Cross for pulling three of his comrades out of their burning tank. He was killed at the battle of El Alamein and his named is carved on the school war memorial, a fitting gesture to the great democracy of death.

And the yo-yo? I replaced it in the box among the school reports, the old essays and those letters from my parents which I thought might interest my son or my grandchildren. Finding it, will he briefly wonder what happy childhood memory made an old man so reluctant to throw it away?

The Victim

You know Princess Ilsa Mancelli, of course. I mean by that that you must have seen her on the cinema screen; on television; pictured in newspapers arriving at airports with her latest husband; relaxing on their yacht; bejewelled at first nights, gala nights, at any night and in any place where it is obligatory for the rich and successful to show themselves. Even if, like me, you have nothing but bored contempt for what I believe is called the international jet set, you can hardly live in the modern world and not know Ilsa Mancelli. And you can't fail to have picked up some scraps about her past. The brief and not particularly successful screen career, when even her heart-stopping beauty couldn't quite compensate for the paucity of talent; the succession of marriages – first to the producer who made her first film and who broke a twenty-year-old marriage to get her; then to a Texan millionaire; lastly to a prince. About two months ago I saw a nauseatingly sentimental picture of her with her two-day-old son in a Rome nursing home. So it looks as if this marriage, sanctified as it is by wealth, a title and maternity, may be intended as her final adventure.

The husband before the film producer is, I notice, no

longer mentioned. Perhaps her publicity agent fears that a violent death in the family, particularly an unsolved violent death, might tarnish her bright image. Blood and beauty. In the early stages of her career they hadn't been able to resist that cheap, vicarious thrill. But not now. Nowadays her early history, before she married the film producer, has become a little obscure, although there is a suggestion of poor but decent parentage and early struggles suitably rewarded. I am the most obscure part of that obscurity. Whatever you know, or think you know, of Ilsa Mancelli, you won't have heard about me. The publicity machine has decreed that I be name-less, faceless, unremembered, that I no longer exist. Ironically, the machine is right; in any real sense, I don't.

I married her when she was Elsie Bowman aged seventeen. I was assistant librarian at our local branch library and fifteen years older, a thirty-two-year-old virgin, a scholar manqué, thin-faced, a little stooping, my meagre hair already thinning. She worked on the cosmetic counter of our High Street store. She was beautiful then, but with a delicate, tentative, unsophisti-cated loveliness which gave little promise of the polished mature beauty which is hers today. Our story was very ordinary. She returned a book to the library one evening when I was on counter duty. We chatted. She asked my advice about novels for her mother. I spent as long as I dared finding suitable romances for her on the shelves.

I tried to interest her in the books I liked. I asked her about herself, her life, her ambitions. She was the only woman I had been able to talk to. I was enchanted by her, totally and completely besotted.

I used to take my lunch early and make surreptitious visits to the store, watching her from the shadow of a neighbouring pillar. There is one picture which even now seems to stop my heart. She had dabbed her wrist with scent and was holding out a bare arm over the counter so that a prospective customer could smell the perfume. She was entirely absorbed, her young face gravely preoccupied. I watched her, silently, and felt the tears smarting my eyes.

It was a miracle when she agreed to marry me. Her mother (she had no father) was reconciled if not enthusiastic about the match. She didn't, as she made it abundantly plain, consider me much of a catch. But I had a good job with prospects; I was educated; I was steady and reliable; I spoke with a grammar-school accent which, while she affected to deride it, raised my status in her eyes. Besides, any marriage for Elsie was better than none. I was dimly aware when I bothered to think about Elsie in relation to anyone but myself that she and her mother didn't get on.

Mrs Bowman made, as she described it, a splash. There was a full choir and a peal of bells. The church hall was hired and a sit-down meal, ostentatiously unsuitable and badly cooked, was served to eighty guests. Between the pangs of nervousness and indigestion I was conscious of smirking waiters in short white jackets, a couple of giggling bridesmaids from the store, their freckled arms bulging from pink taffeta sleeves, hearty male relatives, red-faced and with buttonholes of carnation and waving fern, who made indelicate jokes and clapped me painfully between the shoulders. There were speeches and warm champagne. And, in the middle of it all, Elsie, my Elsie, like a white rose.

I suppose that it was stupid of me to imagine that I could hold her. The mere sight of our morning faces, smiling at each other's reflection in the bedroom mirror, should have warned me that it couldn't last. But, poor deluded fool, I never dreamed that I might lose her except by death. Her death I dared not contemplate, and I was afraid for the first time of my own. Happiness had made a coward of me. We moved into a new bungalow, chosen by Elsie, sat in new chairs chosen by Elsie, slept in a befrilled bed chosen by Elsie. I was so happy that it was like passing into a new phase of existence, breathing a different air, seeing the most ordinary things as if they were newly created. One isn't necessarily humble when greatly in love. Is it so unreasonable to recognise the value of a love like mine, to believe that the beloved is equally sustained and transformed by it?

She said that she wasn't ready to start a baby and,

without her job, she was easily bored. She took a brief training in shorthand and typing at our local technical college and found herself a position as shorthand typist at the firm of Collingford and Major. That, at least, was how the job started. Shorthand typist, then secretary to Mr Rodney Collingford, then personal secretary, then confidential personal secretary; in my bemused state of uxorious bliss I only half-registered her progress from occasionally taking his dictation when his then secretary was absent to flaunting his gifts of jewellery and sharing his bed.

He was everything I wasn't. Rich (his father had made a fortune from plastics shortly after the war and had left the factory to his only son), coarsely handsome in a swarthy fashion, big-muscled, confident, attractive to women. He prided himself on taking what he wanted. Elsie must have been one of his easiest pickings.

Why, I still wonder, did he want to marry her? I thought at the time that he couldn't resist depriving a pathetic, underprivileged, unattractive husband of a prize which neither looks nor talent had qualified him to deserve. I've noticed that about the rich and successful. They can't bear to see the undeserving prosper. I thought that half the satisfaction for him was in taking her away from me. That was partly why I knew that I had to kill him. But now I'm not so sure. I may have done him an injustice. It may have been both simpler and more complicated than that. She was, you see – she still is – so very beautiful.

I understand her better now. She was capable of kindness, good humour, generosity even, provided she was getting what she wanted. At the time we married, and perhaps eighteen months afterwards, she wanted me. Neither her egoism nor her curiosity had been able to resist such a flattering, overwhelming love. But, for her, marriage wasn't permanency. It was the first and necessary step towards the kind of life she dreamt of and meant to have. She was kind to me, in bed and out, while I was what she wanted. But when she wanted someone else, then my need of her, my jealousy, my bitterness, she saw as a cruel and wilful denial of her basic right – the right to have what she wanted. After all, I'd had her for nearly three years. It was two years more than I had any right to expect. She thought so. Her darling Rodney thought so. When my acquaintances at the library learnt of the divorce I could see in their eyes that they thought so too. And she couldn't see what I was so bitter about. Rodney was perfectly happy to be the guilty party; they weren't, she pointed out caustically, expecting me to behave like a gentleman. I wouldn't have to pay for the divorce. Rodney would see to that. I wasn't being asked to provide her with alimony. Rodney had more than enough. At one point she came close to bribing me with Rodney's money to let her go without fuss.

And yet – was it really as simple as that? She had loved me, or at least needed me, for a time. Had she perhaps seen in me the father that she had lost at five years old?

During the divorce, through which I was, as it were, gently processed by highly paid legal experts as if I were an embarrassing but expendable nuisance to be got rid of with decent speed, I was only able to keep sane by the knowledge that I was going to kill Collingford. I knew that I couldn't go on living in a world where he breathed the same air. My mind fed voraciously on the thought of his death, savoured it, began systematically and with dreadful pleasure to plan it.

A successful murder depends on knowing your victim, his character, his daily routine, his weaknesses, those unalterable and betraying habits which make up the core of personality. I knew quite a lot about Rodney Collingford. I knew facts which Elsie had let fall in her first weeks with the firm, typing-pool gossip. I knew the fuller and rather more intimate facts which she had disclosed in those early days of her enchantment with him, when neither prudence nor kindness had been able to conceal her obsessive preoccupation with her new boss. I should have been warned then. I knew, none better, the need to talk about the absent lover.

What did I know about him? I knew the facts that were common knowledge, of course. That he was wealthy, aged thirty, a notable amateur golfer; that

stentatious mock Georgian house on
e Thames looked after by overpaid but
staff; that he owned a cabin cruiser; that he
r six feet tall; that he was a good business-
eputedly close-fisted; that he was methodical
in h.. bits. I knew a miscellaneous and unrelated set
of facts about him, some of which would be useful, some
important, some of which I couldn't use. I knew – and
this was rather surprising – that he was good with his
hands and liked making things in metal and wood. He
had built an expensively equipped and large workroom
in the grounds of his house and spent every Thursday
evening working there alone. He was a man addicted
to routine. This creativity, however mundane and triv-
ial, I found intriguing, but I didn't let myself dwell on
it. I was interested in him only so far as his personality
and habits were relevant to his death. I never thought of
him as a human being. He had no existence for me apart
from my hate. He was Rodney Collingford, my victim.

First, I decided on the weapon. A gun would have
been the most certain, I supposed, but I didn't know how
to get one and was only too well aware that I wouldn't
know how to load or use it if I did. Besides, I was reading a number of books about murder at the time and I
realised that guns, however cunningly obtained, were
easy to trace. And there was another thing. A gun was
too impersonal, too remote. I wanted to make physical

contact at the moment of death. I wanted to get close enough to see that final look of incredulity and horror as he recognised, simultaneously, me and his death. I wanted to drive a knife into his throat.

I bought it two days after the divorce. I was in no hurry to kill Collingford. I knew that I must take my time, must be patient, if I were to act in safety. One day, perhaps when we were old, I might tell Elsie. But I didn't intend to be found out. This was to be the perfect murder. And that meant taking my time. He would be allowed to live for a full year. But I knew that the earlier I bought the knife the more difficult it would be, twelve months later, to trace the purchase. I didn't buy it locally. I went one Saturday morning by train and bus to a north-east suburb and found a busy ironmongers and general store just off the High Street. There was a variety of knives on display. The blade of the one I selected was about six inches long and was made of strong steel screwed into a plain wooden handle. I think it was probably meant for cutting lino. In the shop its razor-sharp edge was protected by a thick cardboard sheath. It felt good and right in my hand. I stood in a small queue at the pay desk and the cashier didn't even glance up as he took my notes and pushed the change towards me.

But the most satisfying part of my planning was the second stage. I wanted Collingford to suffer. I wanted him to know that he was going to die. It wasn't enough that he should realise it in a last second before I drove in the knife or in that final second before he ceased to know anything for ever. Two seconds of agony, however horrible, weren't an adequate return for what he had done to me. I wanted him to know that he was a condemned man, to know it with increasing certainty, to wonder every morning whether this might be his last day. What if this knowledge did make him cautious, put him on his guard? In this country, he couldn't go armed. He couldn't carry on his business with a hired protector always at his side. He couldn't bribe the police to watch him every moment of the day. Besides, he wouldn't want to be thought a coward. I guessed that he would carry on, outwardly normal, as if the threats were unreal or derisory, something to laugh about with his drinking cronies. He was the sort to laugh at danger. But he would never be sure. And, by the end, his nerve and confidence would be broken. Elsie wouldn't know him for the man she had married.

I would have liked to have telephoned him, but that, I knew, was impracticable. Calls could be traced; he might refuse to talk to me; I wasn't confident that I could disguise my voice. So the sentence of death would have to be sent by post. Obviously, I couldn't write the notes or the envelopes myself. My studies in murder had shown me how difficult it was to disguise handwriting, and the method of cutting out and sticking together letters from a newspaper seemed messy, very time consuming and difficult to manage wearing gloves. I knew, too, that it would be fatal to use my own small portable typewriter or one of the machines at the library. The forensic experts could identify a machine.

And then I hit on my plan. I began to spend my Saturdays and occasional half-days journeying round London and visiting shops where they sold second-hand typewriters. I expect you know the kind of shop; a variety of machines of different ages, some practically obsolete, others hardly used, arranged on tables where the prospective purchaser may try them out. There were new machines too, and the proprietor was usually employed in demonstrating their merits or discussing hire-purchase terms. The customers wandered desultorily around, inspecting the machines, stopping occasionally to type out an exploratory passage. There were little pads of rough paper stacked ready for use. I didn't, of course, use the scrap paper provided. I came supplied with my own writing materials, a well-known brand sold in every stationers and on every railway bookstall. I bought a small supply of paper and envelopes once every two months and never from the same shop. Always, when handling them, I wore a thin pair of gloves, slipping them on as soon as my typing was complete. If someone were near, I would tap out the usual drivel about the sharp brown fox or all good men coming to the aid of the party. But if I were quite alone I would type something very different.

'This is the first comunication, Collingford. You'll be getting them regularly from now on. They're just to let you know that I'm going to kill you.'

'You can't escape me, Collingford. Don't bother to inform the police. They can't help you.'

'I'm getting nearer, Collingford. Have you made your will?'

'Not long now, Collingford. What does it feel like to be under sentence of death?'

The warnings weren't particularly elegant. As a librarian, I could think of a number of apt quotations which would have added a touch of individuality or style, perhaps even of sardonic humour, to the bald sentence of death. But I dared not risk originality. The notes had to be ordinary, the kind of threat which any-one of his enemies, a worker, a competitor, a cuckolded husband, might have sent.

Sometimes I had a lucky day. The shop would be large, well supplied, nearly empty. I would be able to move from typewriter to typewriter and leave with perhaps a dozen or so notes and addressed envelopes ready to send. I always carried a folded newspaper in which I could conceal my writing pad and envelopes and into which I could quickly slip my little stock of typed messages.

It was quite a job to keep myself supplied with notes and I discovered interesting parts of London and fascinating shops. I particularly enjoyed this part of my plan. I wanted Collingford to get two notes a week, one posted on Sunday and one on Thursday. I wanted him to come to dread Friday and Monday mornings when the familiar typed envelope would drop on his mat. I wanted him to believe the threat was real. And why should he not believe it? How could the force of my hate and resolution not transmit itself through paper and typescript to his gradually comprehending brain?

I wanted to keep an eye on my victim. It shouldn't have been difficult; we lived in the same town. But our lives were worlds apart. He was a hard and sociable drinker. I never went inside a public house, and would have been particularly ill at ease in the kind of public house he frequented. But, from time to time, I would see him in the town. Usually he would be parking his Jaguar, and I would watch his quick, almost furtive look to left and right before he turned to lock the door. Was it my imagination that he seemed older, that some of the confidence had drained out of him?

Once, when walking by the river on a Sunday in early spring, I saw him manoeuvring his boat through Teddington Lock. Ilsa – she had, I knew, changed her name after her marriage – was with him. She was wearing a white trouser suit; her flowing hair was bound by a red scarf. There was a party. I could see two more men and a couple of girls and hear high female squeals of laughter. I turned quickly and slouched away as if I were the guilty one. But not before I had seen Collingford's face. This time I couldn't be mistaken. It wasn't, surely, the tedious job of getting his boat unscratched through the lock that made him appear so grey and strained.

The third phase of my planning meant moving house. I wasn't sorry to go. The bungalow, feminine, chintzy, smelling of fresh paint and the new shoddy furniture which she had chosen, was Elsie's home not mine. Her scent still lingered in cupboards and on pillows. In these inappropriate surroundings I had known greater happiness than I was ever to know again. But now I paced restlessly from room to empty room, fretting to be gone.

It took me four months to find the house I wanted. It had to be on or very near to the river within two or three miles upstream of Collingford's house. It had to be small and reasonably cheap. Money wasn't too much of a difficulty. It was a time of rising house prices and the modern bungalow sold at three hundred pounds more than I had paid for it. I could get another mortgage without difficulty if I didn't ask for too much, but I thought it likely that, for what I wanted, I should have to pay cash.

The house agents perfectly understood that a man on his own found a three-bedroom bungalow too large for him and, even if they thought me rather vague about my new requirements and irritatingly imprecise about the reasons for rejecting their offerings, they still sent me orders to view. And then, suddenly on an afternoon in April, I found exactly what I was looking for. It actually stood on the river, separated from it only by a narrow towpath. It was a one-bedroom, shack-like wooden bungalow with a tiled roof, set in a small neglected plot of sodden grass and overgrown flower beds. There had once been a wooden landing stage but now the two remaining planks, festooned with weeds and tags of rotted rope, were half-submerged beneath the slime of the river. The paint on the small veranda had long ago flaked away. The wallpaper of twined roses in the sitting room was blotched and faded. The previous owner had left two old cane chairs and a ramshackle table. The kitchen was pokey and ill-equipped. Everywhere there hung a damp miasma of depression and decay. In summer, when the neighbouring shacks and bungalows were occupied by holidaymakers and weekenders, it would, no doubt, be cheerful enough. But in October, when I planned to kill Collingford, it would be as deserted and isolated as a disused morgue. I bought it and paid cash. I was even able to knock two hundred pounds off the asking price.

My life that summer was almost happy. I did my job at the library adequately. I lived alone in the shack, looking after myself as I had before my marriage. I spent my evenings watching television. The images flickered in front of my eyes almost unregarded, a monochrome background to my bloody and obsessive thoughts.

I practised with the knife until it was as familiar in my hand as an eating utensil. Collingford was taller than me by six inches. The thrust then would have to be upward. It made a difference to the way I held the knife and I experimented to find the most comfortable and effective grip. I hung a bolster on a hook in the bedroom door and lunged at a marked spot for hours at a time. Of course, I didn't actually insert the knife; nothing must dull the sharpness of its blade. Once a week, a special treat, I sharpened it to an even keener edge.

Two days after moving into the bungalow I bought a dark-blue untrimmed tracksuit and a pair of light running shoes. Throughout the summer I spent an occasional evening running on the towpath. The people who owned the neighbouring chalets – when they were there, which was infrequently – got used to the sound of my television through the closed curtains and the sight of my figure jogging past their windows. I kept apart from them and from everyone, and summer passed into autumn. The shutters were put up on all the chalets except mine. The towpath became mushy with fallen leaves. Dusk fell early, and the summer sights and sounds died on the river. And it was October.

He was due to die on Thursday October 17th, the anniversary of the final decree of divorce. It had to be a Thursday, the evening which he spent by custom alone in his workshop, but it was a particularly happy augury that the anniversary should fall on this day. I knew that he would be there. Every Thursday for nearly a year I had padded along the two and a half miles of the footpath in the evening dusk and had stood briefly watching the squares of light from his windows and the dark bulk of the house behind.

It was a warm evening. There had been a light drizzle for most of the day but, by dusk, the skies had cleared. There was a thin white sliver of moon and it cast a trembling ribbon of light across the river. I left the library at my usual time, said my usual goodnights. I knew that I had been my normal self during the day, solitary, occasionally a little sarcastic, conscientious, betraying no hint of the inner tumult.

I wasn't hungry when I got home but I made myself eat an omelette and drink two cups of coffee. I put on my swimming trunks and hung around my neck a plastic toilet bag containing the knife. Over the trunks I put on my track suit, slipping a pair of thin rubber gloves into the pocket. Then, at about quarter past seven, I left the shack and began my customary gentle trot along the tow path.

When I got to the chosen spot opposite to Collingford's

house I could see at once that all was well. The house was in darkness but there were the expected lighted windows of his workshop. I saw that the cabin cruiser was moored against the boathouse. I stood very still and listened. There was no sound. Even the light breeze had died and the yellowing leaves on the riverside elms hung motionless. The towpath was completely deserted. I slipped into the shadow of the hedge where the trees grew thickest and found the place I had already selected. I put on the rubber gloves, slipped out of the tracksuit, and left it folded around my running shoes in the shadow of the hedge. Then, still watching carefully to left and right, I made my way to the river.

I knew just where I must enter and leave the water. I had selected a place where the bank curved gently, where the water was shallow and the bottom was firm and comparatively free of mud. The water struck very cold, but I expected that. Every night during that autumn I had bathed in cold water to accustom my body to the shock. I swam across the river with my methodical but quiet breaststroke, hardly disturbing the dark surface of the water. I tried to keep out of the path of moonlight but, from time to time, I swam into its silver gleam and saw my red gloved hands parting in front of me as if they were already stained with blood.

I used Collingford's landing stage to clamber out the other side. Again I stood still and listened. There was no sound except for the constant moaning of the river and the solitary cry of a night bird. I made my way silently over the grass. Outside the door of his workroom, I paused again. I could hear the noise of some kind of machinery. I wondered whether the door would be locked, but it opened easily when I turned the handle. I moved into a blaze of light.

I knew exactly what I had to do. I was perfectly calm. It was over in about four seconds. I don't think he really had a chance. He was absorbed in what he had been doing, bending over a lathe, and the sight of an almost naked man, walking purposely towards him, left him literally impotent with surprise. But, after that first paralysing second, he knew me. Oh yes, he knew me! Then I drew my right hand from behind my back and struck. The knife went in as sweetly as if the flesh had been butter. He staggered and fell. I had expected that and I let myself go loose and fell on top of him. His eyes were glazed, his mouth opened and there was a gush of dark red blood. I twisted the knife viciously in the wound, relishing the sound of tearing sinews. Then I waited. I counted five deliberately, then raised myself from his prone figure and crouched behind him before withdrawing the knife. When I withdrew it there was a fountain of sweet-smelling blood which curved from his throat like an arch. There is one thing I shall never forget. The blood must have been red, what other colour could it have been? But, at the time and for ever afterwards, I saw it as a golden stream.

I checked my body for bloodstains before I left the workshop and rinsed my arms under the cold tap at his sink. My bare feet made no marks on the wooden-block flooring. I closed the door quietly after me and, once again, stood listening. Still no sound. The house was dark and empty.

The return journey was more exhausting than I had thought possible. The river seemed to have widened and I thought that I should never reach my home shore. I was glad I had chosen a shallow part of the stream and that the bank was firm. I doubt whether I could have drawn myself up through a welter of mud and slime. I was shivering violently as I zipped up my tracksuit, and it took me precious seconds to get on my running shoes. After I had run about a mile down the towpath I weighted the toilet bag containing the knife with stones from the path and hurled it into the middle of the river. I guessed that they would drag part of the Thames for the weapon but they could hardly search the whole stream. And, even if they did, the toilet bag was one sold at the local chain store which anyone might have bought, and I was confident that the knife could never be traced to me. Half an hour later I was back in my shack. I had left the television on and the news was just ending. I made myself a cup of hot cocoa and sat to watch it. I felt drained of thought and energy as if I had just made love. I was conscious of nothing but my tiredness, my body's coldness gradually returning to life in the warmth of the electric fire, and a great peace.

He must have had quite a lot of enemies. It was nearly a fortnight before the police got round to interviewing me. Two officers came, a Detective Inspector and a Sergeant, both in plain clothes. The Sergeant did most of the talking; the other just sat, looking round at the sitting room, glancing out at the river, looking at the two of us from time to time from cold grey eyes as if the whole investigation were a necessary bore. The Sergeant said the usual reassuring platitudes about just a few questions. I was nervous, but that didn't worry me. They would expect me to be nervous. I told myself that, whatever I did, I mustn't try to be clever. I mustn't talk too much. I had decided to tell them that I spent the whole evening watching television, confident that no one would be able to refute this. I knew that no friends would have called on me. I doubted whether my colleagues at the library even knew where I lived. And I had no telephone so I need not fear that a caller's ring had gone unanswered during that crucial hour and a half.

On the whole it was easier than I had expected. Only once did I feel myself at risk. That was when the Inspector suddenly intervened. He said in a harsh voice:

'He married your wife didn't he? Took her away from you some people might say. Nice piece of goods, too, by the look of her. Didn't you feel any grievance? Or was it all nice and friendly? You take her, old chap. No ill feelings. That kind of thing.'

It was hard to accept the contempt in his voice but if he hoped to provoke me he didn't succeed. I had been expecting this question. I was prepared. I looked down at my hands and waited a few seconds before I spoke. I knew exactly what I would say.

'I could have killed Collingford myself when she first told me about him. But I had to come to terms with it. She went for the money you see. And if that's the kind of wife you have, well she's going to leave you sooner or later. Better sooner than when you have a family. You tell yourself "good riddance". I don't mean I felt that at first, of course. But I did feel it in the end. Sooner than I expected, really.'

That was all I said about Elsie then or ever. They came back three times. They asked if they could look round my shack. They looked round it. They took away two of my suits and the tracksuit for examination. Two weeks later they returned them without comment. I never knew what they suspected, or even if they did suspect. Each time they came I said less, not more. I never varied my story. I never allowed them to provoke me into discussing my marriage or speculating about the crime. I just sat there, telling them the same thing over and over again. I never felt in any real danger. I knew that they had dragged some lengths of the river but that they hadn't found the weapon. In the end they gave up. I always had the feeling that I was pretty low on their list of suspects and that, by the end, their visits were merely a matter of form.

It was three months before Elsie came to me. I was glad that it wasn't earlier. It might have looked suspicious if she had arrived at the shack when the police were with me. After Collingford's death I hadn't seen her. There were pictures of her in the national and local newspapers, fragile in sombre furs and black hat at the inquest, bravely controlled at the crematorium, sitting in her drawing room in afternoon dress and pearls with her husband's dog at her feet, the personification of loneliness and grief.

'I can't think who could have done it. He must have been a madman. Rodney hadn't an enemy in the world.'

That statement caused some ribald comment at the library. One of the assistants said, 'He's left her a fortune I hear. Lucky for her she had an alibi. She was at a London theatre all the evening, watching *Macbeth*. Otherwise, from what I've heard of our Rodney Collingford, people might have started to get ideas about his fetching little widow.'

Then he gave me a sudden embarrassed glance,

remembering who the widow was.

And so one Friday evening, she came. She drove herself and was alone. The dark green Saab pulled up to my ramshackle gate. She came into the sitting room and looked around in a kind of puzzled contempt. After a moment, still not speaking, she sat in one of the fireside chairs and crossed her legs, moving one caressingly against the other. I hadn't seen her sitting like that before. She looked up at me. I was standing stiffly in front of her chair, my lips dry. When I spoke I couldn't recognise my own voice.

'So you've come back?' I said.

She stared at me, incredulous, and then she laughed:

'To you? Back for keeps? Don't be silly, darling! I've just come to pay a visit. Besides, I wouldn't dare to come back, would I? I might be frightened that you'd stick a knife into my throat.'

I couldn't speak. I stared at her, feeling the blood drain from my face. Then I heard her high, rather childish voice. It sounded almost kind.

'Don't worry, I shan't tell. You were right about him, darling, you really were. He wasn't at all nice really. And mean! I didn't care so much about your meanness. After all, you don't earn so very much, do you? But he had half a million! Think of it, darling. I've been left half a million! And he was so mean that he expected me to go on working as his secretary even after we were married. I typed all his letters! I really did! All that he sent from home, anyway. And I had to open his post every morning unless the envelopes had a secret little sign on them he'd told his friends about to show that they were private.'

I said through bloodless lips.

'So all my notes—'

'He never saw them, darling. Well, I didn't want to worry him, did I? And I knew they were from you. I knew when the first one arrived. You never could spell communication, could you? I noticed that when you used to write to the house agents and the solicitor before we were married. It made me laugh considering that you're an educated librarian and I was only a shop assistant.'

'So you knew all the time. You knew that it was going to happen.'

'Well, I thought that it might. But he really was horrible, darling. You can't imagine. And now I've got half a million! Isn't it lucky that I have an alibi? I thought you might come on that Thursday. And Rodney never did enjoy a serious play.'

After that brief visit I never saw or spoke to her again. I stayed in the shack, but life became pointless after Collingford's death. Planning his murder had been an interest, after all. Without Elsie and without my victim there seemed little point in living. And, about a year after his death, I began to dream. I still dream, always on a Monday and Friday. I live through it all again; the noiseless run along the towpath over the mush of damp leaves; the quiet swim across the river; the silent opening of his door; the upward thrust of the knife; the vicious turn in the wound; the animal sound of tearing tissues; the curving stream of golden blood. Only the homeward swim is different. In my dream the river is no longer a cleansing stream, luminous under the sickle moon, but a cloying, impenetrable, slow-moving bog of viscous blood through which I struggle in impotent panic towards a steadily receding shore.

I know about the significance of the dream. I've read all about the psychology of guilt. Since I lost Elsie I've done all my living through books. But it doesn't help. And I no longer know who I am. I know who I used to be, our local assistant librarian, gentle, scholarly, timid, Elsie's husband. But then I killed Collingford. The man I was couldn't have done that. He wasn't that kind of person. So who am I? It isn't really surprising, I suppose, that the library committee suggested so tactfully that I ought to look for a less exacting job. A less exacting job than the post of assistant librarian? But you can't blame them. No one can be efficient and keep his mind on the job when he doesn't know who he is.

Sometimes, when I'm in a public house – and I seem to spend most of my time there nowadays since I've been out of work – I'll look over someone's shoulder at a newspaper photograph of Elsie and say:

'That's the beautiful Ilsa Mancelli. I was her first husband.'

I've got used to the way people sidle away from me, the ubiquitous pub bore, their eyes averted, their voices suddenly hearty. But sometimes, perhaps because they've been lucky with the horses and feel a spasm of pity for a poor deluded sod, they push a few coins over the counter to the barman before making their way to the door, and buy me a drink.

The Murder of Santa Claus

If you're an addict of detective fiction you may have heard of me, Charles Mickledore. I say addict advisably; no occasional or highly discriminating reader of the genre is likely to ask for my latest offering at his public library. I'm no H. R. F. Keating, no Dick Francis, not even a P. D. James. But I do a workmanlike job on the old conventions, for those who like their murders cosy, and, although my amateur detective, the Hon. Martin Carstairs, has been described as a pallid copy of Peter Wimsey, at least I haven't burdened him with a monocle, or with Harriet Vane for that matter. I make enough to augment a modest private income. Unmarried, solitary, unsociable; why should I expect my writing to be any more successful than my life?

Sometimes I'm even asked to do a radio chat show when one of the more distinguished practitioners of death isn't available. I've got used to the old question: have you ever, Mr Mickledore, had personal experience of murder? Invariably I lie. For one thing, interviewers never expect the truth; there isn't time. And for another, they wouldn't believe me. The murder I was involved with was as complicated, as bizarre as any fictional mayhem I've managed to concoct, even in my more inspired moments. If I were writing about it I'd call it 'The Murder of Santa Claus'. And that, essentially, was what it was.

Appropriately enough, it took place in the heyday of the cosy 'whodunnits', the Christmas of 1939, the first Christmas of the war. I was sixteen, an awkward age at the best of times, and, as a sensitive and solitary only child, I was more awkward than most. My father was in the Colonial Service serving in Singapore, and I usually spent the winter holiday with my housemaster and his family. But this year my parents wrote that my father's elder half-brother, Victor Mickledore, had invited me to his Cotswold manor house at Marston Turville. His instructions were precise. I was to arrive by the 4.15 train on Christmas Eve and would depart on the morning of Wednesday December 27th. I would be met at Marston station by his housekeeper/secretary, Miss Makepiece. There would be four other guests: Major and Mrs Turville, from whom he had bought the manor five years previously; his stepson Henry Caldwell, the famous amateur flyer; and the actress Miss Gloria Belsize. I had, of course, heard of Caldwell and of Miss Belsize although I don't suppose that even I, naive as I was, supposed it to be her real name.

My uncle – or should it be step-uncle? – apologised for the fact that there would be no other young guests to keep me company. That didn't worry me. But the thought of the visit did. I had only met my uncle once, when I was ten. I had the idea, gleaned as children do from half-spoken sentences and overheard remarks, that my parents and he were on bad terms. I think he had once wanted to marry my mother. Perhaps this was an attempt at reconciliation now that war, with its uncertainties, had started. My father had made it plain in his letter that I was expected to accept the invitation and that he was relying on me to make a good impression. I put out of my mind the treacherous thought that my uncle was very rich and that he had no children.

Miss Makepiece was waiting for me at Marston station. She greeted me with no particular warmth, and as she led the way to the waiting Daimler I was reminded of the school matron on one of her more repressive days. We drove through the village in silence. It lay sombre and deserted in its pre-Christmas calm. I can remember the church half-hidden behind the great yews and the silent school with the children's Christmas chains of coloured paper gleaming dully against the windows.

Marston Turville is a small seventeenth-century manor house, its three wings built round a courtyard. I saw it first as a mass of grey stone, blacked out as was the whole village, under low broken clouds. My uncle greeted me before a log fire in the great hall. I came in, blinking, from the December dusk into a blaze of colour; candles sparkling on the huge Christmas tree, its tub piled with imitation snowballs of frosted cotton wool; the leaping fire; the gleam of firelight on silver. My fellow guests were taking tea and I see them as a tableau, cups halfway to their lips, predestined victims waiting for the tragedy to begin.

Memory, perverse and selective, has even clothed them appropriately. When I picture that Christmas Eve, I see Henry Caldwell, that doomed hero, in his RAF uniform with his medal ribbons on his breast. But he couldn't have been wearing it. He was only then waiting to report for his RAF training. And I invariably picture Gloria Belsize in the slinky golden evening dress which she changed into for dinner, her nipples pointing the satin; I found it difficult to keep my eyes from them. I see the plain, intimidatingly efficient Miss Makepiece in her grey woollen dress severe as a uniform, the Turvilles in their shabby country tweeds, my uncle always in his immaculate dinner jacket.

He bent over me with his dark sardonic face.

'So you're Alison's boy. I wondered how you'd turn out.'

I thought I knew what he was thinking; that the right father would have made all the difference. I was aware of my lack of height beside his six-foot two – only Henry could match him – and of my adolescent crop of pimples. He introduced me to my fellow guests.

The Turvilles were a gentle-faced white-haired couple, older than I had expected and both rather deaf. I found Henry's austere good looks rather formidable; shyness and hero-worship made me dumb. Miss Belsize's face was known to me from the papers. Now I saw what tactful touching-up had concealed; the deepening lines under the eyes, the sagging jawline, the hectic flush under the remarkable eyes. Then I wondered why she should be so excited by Christmas. Now I realise that she was half-drunk for most of the day and that my uncle saw it, was amused by it, and made no attempt to curb her. We were an ill-assorted party. None of us was at ease, myself least of all. After that first greeting my uncle hardly spoke to me. But whenever we were together I was aware of his intense scrutiny, of being in some way under approval.

The first intimation of horror, the Christmas cracker with its message of menace, was delivered at seven o'clock. It was a long tradition at Marston Turville that carol singers from the village sang to their squire on Christmas Eve. They arrived promptly, sidling in under the blackout curtain one by one, as the lights in the great hall were lowered. There were ten of them, seven men and three women, cloaked against the cold of that frosty night, and each carrying a lantern which was lit as soon as the heavy door was closed. I stood, uneasy in my newly acquired dinner jacket, between Mrs Turville and Henry to the right of the fire and listened to the old, innocently nostalgic carols resolutely sung in their hearty country voices. Afterwards the butler, Poole, and one of the maids brought in mince pies and hot punch. But there was an air of constraint. They should have been singing for the Turvilles. The manor was in alien hands. They ate and drank with almost unseemly haste. The lights were put out, the door opened, and my uncle with Miss Makepiece at his side thanked them and said goodnight. Miss Belsize fluttered round them as they left, almost as if she were chatelaine of the manor. The Turvilles had stood distanced at the far end of the room and, when the singing began, I saw her hand steal out to his.

We saw the cracker almost at once. It had been placed on a small table near the door. It was fashioned of red and yellow crêpe paper, overlarge, obviously an amateur effort but made with some skill. Miss Belsize seized it and read:

'Victor Mickledore! It's got your name on it, darling. Someone's left you a present. What fun! Do let's pull it!'

He didn't respond but drew on his cigarette and gazed at her contemptuously through the smoke. She flushed, then held the cracker out to me and we pulled together. The paper tore apart without a bang and a small object fell out and rolled over the carpet. I bent and picked it up. Wrapped neatly in an oblong of paper was a small metal charm in the shape of a skull attached to a keyring; I had seen similar ones in gift shops. I opened the paper folded round it and saw a verse hand-printed in capitals. Gloria cried:

'Read it out, darling!'

I glanced at my uncle's impassive face and heard my nervous, overloud voice:

> *'Merry Christmas, Mickledore!*
> *Go to bed and sleep no more.*
> *Take this charm and hold it fast;*
> *This night's sleep shall be your last.*
> *Christmas bells ring merrily;*
> *Bells of hell shall ring for thee.*
> *Happy Christmas, Mickledore.*
> *Go to bed and sleep no more.'*

There was a moment's silence, Then Henry said calmly, 'One of your neighbours doesn't like you, Victor. He's wrong about the bells, though. No Christmas bells in wartime. The bells of hell are another matter. No doubt they aren't subject to Defence Regulations.'

Gloria's voice was piercing: 'It's a death threat! Someone wants to kill you. That woman was among the singers, wasn't she? The one whose child you ran over and killed last Christmas Eve. The village schoolmistress. Saunders. That's her name. Mrs Saunders was here!'

There was a dreadful silence. My uncle spoke in a voice like a whiplash: 'A witness saw a dark Daimler but it wasn't mine. My Daimler never left the garage last Christmas Eve. Poole confirmed it.'

'I know, darling. I didn't mean anything . . .'

'You seldom do.' He turned to Poole:

'The best place for this is the kitchen grate.'

Then Henry spoke: 'I shouldn't destroy it, not for a time anyway. It's harmless enough, but if you get another and the thing becomes a nuisance it might be as well to let the police see it.'

Miss Makepiece said in her cool voice, 'I'll put it in the study desk'.

She took it away and the rest of us followed her with our eyes. Gloria said, 'But you'll lock your door, darling. I think you ought to lock your bedroom door.'

Victor said, 'I lock my door against no one in my house. If I have an enemy I meet him face to face. And now perhaps we could go in to dinner.'

It was an uncomfortable meal. Gloria's loud, half-tipsy volubility served only to emphasise the general cheerlessness. And it was at dinner that she told me about another of my uncle's traditions. Promptly at one o'clock, 'to give us time to get to sleep or at least be in our proper beds, darling', he would put on a Santa Claus costume and distribute gifts to each of his guests. We would find a stocking ready at the foot of each bed.

'See what I got last year,' she exulted, stretching out her arm to me across the table. The diamond bracelet sparkled in the candlelight. My uncle cracked a walnut in his palm like a pistol shot.

'You may do better this year if you're a good girl.'

The words and the tone were an insult.

I remember the rest of the evening in a series of brightly lit cameos. Dancing after dinner; the Turvilles staidly circling, Gloria clinging amorously to Henry, Miss Makepiece watching with contemptuous eyes from her seat by the fire. Then the game of hunt the hare; according to Henry this was another of Victor's Christmas traditions, one in which the whole household was required to take part. I was chosen as hare. A balloon was tied to my arm and I was given five minutes to hide anywhere in the house. The aim was to regain the front door before I was caught and the balloon punctured. For me it was the only jolly part of the evening. I remember giggling housemaids, Gloria chasing me round the kitchen table, making ineffectual lunges with a rolled magazine, my last mad rush to the door as Henry burst from the study and exploded the balloon with one swipe of a branch of holly. Later, I remember the dying firelight gleaming on crystal decanters as Poole brought in the drinks tray. The Turvilles went to bed first – she wanted to listen to the ten forty-five Epilogue in her own room – and were shortly followed by Gloria and Miss Makepiece. I said my good-nights at eleven forty-five, leaving my uncle alone with Henry, the drinks tray between them.

At my bedroom door I found Miss Makepiece waiting for me. She asked me to change rooms with Henry. He was in the red room with its curtained four-poster and, after his accident in June when he had been forced down in his flight to South America and had escaped in seconds from the blazing cockpit, she thought he might find the bed claustrophobic. She helped me move my few belongings into the new room on the back corridor and bade me goodnight. I can't say I was sorry to be further from my uncle.

Christmas Eve was nearly over. I thought about my day as I undressed and made my way to the bathroom at the turn of the corridor. It hadn't been too bad, after all. Henry had been remote but amiable. Miss Makepiece was intimidating, but she had left me alone. I was still terrified of Victor but Mrs Turville had been a motherly and protective presence. Deaf and shabby, she yet had her own gentle authority. There was a small carved statue of the Virgin in a niche to the right of the fireplace. Before the game of hunt the hare, someone had tied a balloon to its neck. Quietly she had asked Poole to remove it and he had at once obeyed. Afterwards she had explained to me that the statue was called the Turville Grace and for three hundred years had protected the heir from harm. She told me that her only son was in a Guards regiment and asked about my own family. How glad

I must be that they were in Singapore where the war could not touch them. Could not touch them! The irony stings even now.

The lined bed curtains and the canopy were of heavy crimson material, damask I suppose. Because of some defect in the rails they couldn't be fully drawn back except at the foot and there was barely space for my bedside table. Lying on the high and surprisingly hard mattress I had the impression of being enveloped in flames of blood, and I could understand Miss Makepiece's concern that Henry should sleep elsewhere. I don't think I realised then, child that I was, that she was in love with him any more than I accepted what I surely must have known, that Gloria had been my uncle's mistress.

I slept almost immediately, but that internal clock which regulates our waking made me stir after little more than two hours. I switched on my bedside lamp and looked at my watch. It was a minute to one o'clock. Santa Claus would be on his way. I put out the light and waited, feeling again some of the excitement I had felt as a young child on this most magical night of the year. He came promptly, gliding in soundlessly over the carpet. Curtained as I was I could hear nothing, not even the sound of his breathing. I half-covered my head with the sheet, feigned sleep, and watched with one narrowed eye. He was holding a torch and the pool of light shone momentarily on his fur-trimmed robe, the peaked hood drawn forward over his face. A white-gloved hand slipped a package into the stocking. And then he was gone as silently as he had come.

At sixteen, one has no patience. I waited until I was sure he had gone then crept down the bed. The present, wrapped in red striped paper, was slim. I untied the ribbon. Inside was a box containing a gold cigarette case carved with the initials H.R.C. How odd that I hadn't remembered! This present was, of course, meant for Henry. I should have to wait for mine until morning. On impulse I opened the case. Inside was a typed message.

'Happy Christmas! No need to get it tested. It's gold all right. And in case you're beginning to hope, this is the only gold you'll get from me.'

I wished I hadn't opened it, hadn't seen that offensive gibe.

I took some time replacing the wrapping and ribbon as neatly as I could, put the package back in the stocking, and settled myself to sleep.

I woke once again in the night. I needed to go to the lavatory. The corridor, like the whole house, was blacked out but a small oil lamp was kept burning on a table and I groped my sleepy way by its light. I had regained my room when I heard footsteps. I slipped back into the recess of the door and watched. Major and Mrs Turville, dressing-gowned, came silently down the corridor and slipped into the bathroom, furtively as if gaining a refuge. He was carrying what looked like a rolled-up towel. I waited, curious. In a few seconds she put her head round the door, glanced down the passage, then withdrew. Three seconds later they came out together, he still carrying the rolled towel as if it were a baby. Afraid of being detected in my spying, I closed the door. It was a curious incident. But I soon forgot it in oblivion.

I had drawn back my curtain before sleeping and was woken by the first light of dawn. A tall figure was standing at the foot of the bed. It was Henry. He came up to me and handed me a gift-wrapped package saying:

'Sorry if I disturbed you. I was trying to exchange presents before you woke.'

He took his own but didn't open it, and watched while I tore the paper off mine. My uncle had given me a gold watch wrapped in a ten-pound note. The richness of it left me speechless but I knew that I was pink with pleasure. He watched my face then said:

'I wonder what price he'll exact for that. Don't let him corrupt you. That's what he uses his money for, playing with people. Your parents are overseas, aren't they?'

I nodded.

'It might be sensible to write to them that you'd rather not holiday here. It's your affair. I don't want to interfere. But your uncle isn't good for the young. He isn't good for anyone.'

I don't know what, if anything, I should have found to say. I recall my momentary resentment that he should have spoilt some of my pleasure in my present. But it was then that we heard the first scream.

It was horrible, a wild female screeching. Henry ran out and I scrambled out of bed and followed, down the corridor and round to the front of the house. The screams were coming from the open door of my uncle's bedroom. As we reached it, Gloria appeared in the doorway, dishevelled in her mauve silk dressing gown, her hair loose. Clutching at Henry, she stopped screaming, caught her breath and gasped:

'He's dead! Murdered! Victor's murdered!'

We slackened our pace and walked almost slowly up to the bed. I was aware of Miss Makepiece behind us, of Poole coming down the corridor bearing a tray with early morning tea. My uncle lay stretched on his back, still in his Santa Claus costume, the hood framing his face. His mouth was half open in a parody of a grin; his nose was sharply beaked like a bird's; his hands, neatly disposed at his side, seemed unnaturally white and thin, too frail for the heavy signet ring. Everything about him was diminished, made harmless, almost pathetic. But my eyes came back and fixed themselves finally on the knife. It had been plunged into his chest, pinning to it the menacing rhyme from the Christmas cracker.

I felt a dreadful nausea which, to my shame, gave way to a heady mixture of fear and excitement. I was aware of Major Turville coming up beside me. He said, 'I'll tell my wife. She mustn't come in here, Henry you'd better ring the police.'

Miss Makepiece said, 'Is he dead?'

She might have been asking if breakfast was ready.

Henry answered, 'Oh yes, he's dead all right.'

'But there's so little blood. Round the knife. Why didn't he bleed?'

'That means he was dead before the knife was put in.'

I wondered that they could be so calm. Then Henry turned to Poole: 'Is there a key to this room?'

'Yes, Sir. On the keyboard in the business room.'

'Fetch it please. We'd better lock up here and keep out until the police arrive.'

They ignored Gloria, who crouched snivelling at the foot of the bed. And they seemed to have forgotten me. I stood there, shivering, my eyes fixed on that grotesque red-robed corpse which had been Victor Mickledore.

Then Poole coughed, ridiculously deferential: 'I'm wondering, Sir, why he didn't defend himself. Mr Mickledore always kept a gun in the drawer of the bed-side table.'

Henry went over and pulled it open.

It was then that Gloria stopped crying, gave a hysterical laugh, and sang out in a quavering voice:

> *'Happy Christmas, Mickledore,*
> *Go to bed and wake no more.*
> *Merry Christmas, sound the knell,*
> *Murdered, dead and gone to hell.'*

But all our eyes were on the drawer.
It was empty. The gun was missing.

A retired seventy-six-year-old police officer, even from a small County Force, isn't short of memories to solace his fireside evenings and, until Charles Mickledore's letter arrived, I hadn't thought about the Marston Turville killing for years. Mickledore asked me to give my version of the case as part of a private account he was writing, and I was surprised how vividly the memories returned. I don't know how he managed to run me to earth. He mentioned that he wrote detective fiction and that may have helped. Not that I read it. In my experience police officers rarely do. Once you've had to cope with the real thing, you lose the taste for fantasy.

I was interested to learn what had happened to that shy, unattractive, secretive boy. At least he was still alive. Too many of that little group which had spent Christmas Eve 1939 with him at Marston Turville had come to violent ends. One murdered; one shot down in flames; one killed in a car smash; two caught in a London air raid; and one, largely due to my activities, ignominiously dead at the end of a rope. Not that I lose any sleep over that. You get on with your job and let the consequences look after themselves. That's the only way I know to do police work. But I'd better get on with my story.

My name is John Pottinger and in December 1939 I was a newly promoted Detective Inspector. The Mickledore killing was my first murder. I arrived at the manor with my Sergeant at nine thirty and old Doc McKay, the police surgeon, was hard on my heels. Henry Caldwell had taken charge and had done all the correct things. The death room was locked, no one had been allowed to leave the house and they had all kept together. Only Mrs Turville was missing; locked in her bedroom and, according to her husband, too distressed to see me. But the Major was willing to let me in as soon as Doc MacKay had taken a look at her. He was their family doctor; but then, he was doctor to all the village. Most of us involved in the case knew each other. That was my strength; it was also my weakness.

Once we had parted the heavy Santa Claus robe, its inner fold stiffened and darkened with blood, it didn't need the missing gun to tell us that Mickledore had been shot. The bullet had been aimed at short range to the heart. And I couldn't see Mickledore lying there meekly waiting for it. There was an empty glass on his bedside table. Taking it up, I could just detect the faint smell of whisky. But I had an open mind on what else it might have contained.

Doc McKay pulled out the knife – an ordinary sharp-bladed kitchen knife – with one quick jerk of his gloved hand. He sniffed round the larger gunshot wound for signs of scorching, then checked the body temperature and the progress of rigor mortis. The timing of death is always chancy, but he finally estimated that Mickledore had been killed sometime between eleven thirty and two o'clock. It was an opinion that the post-mortem examination subsequently confirmed.

We were short of manpower in that first winter of the phoney war and I had to manage with one Sergeant and a couple of Detective Constables new to the job. I interviewed the suspects myself. It wouldn't have been convincing if they'd pretended any grief and, to give them their due, they didn't try. They spoke the conventional platitudes and so did I; but we didn't fool each other.

Caldwell said that he had last seen Mickledore carrying a glass of whisky to his room when they parted in the corridor shortly before midnight. The Turvilles and Miss Belsize, who had retired earlier, claimed that they were asleep by midnight and hadn't stirred until morning. Charles Mickledore admitted that he had gone to the bathroom sometime after one – he hadn't looked at his watch – but insisted that he had seen no one and heard nothing. I had a strong impression he was lying but I didn't press him at that first interview. The young seldom lie convincingly. They haven't had time to practise like the rest of us.

Poole and the cook, Mrs Banting, lived in separate flats in the stable block; Mickledore had a dislike of servants sleeping in the house. The other three maids were local girls who came in part-time from the village and had gone home after dinner. Mrs Banting had put the turkey and Christmas pudding in the pantry before leaving for her bed at eleven and Poole had left with her. She had returned at six to begin her Christmas preparations and Poole had arrived at seven to take up the early morning tea trays. Both claimed to have spent a night of innocent oblivion and swore that their keys hadn't left their possession. No one heard the gunshot. The Turvilles were deaf, Miss Belsize probably half-drunk and doped, the young sleep soundly, and Mickledore's door was of heavy oak. All the same, it was odd.

I may as well admit that my first suspect was Caldwell. This was a murder requiring nerve and that he had in plenty. I reckoned that his country had a better use for him than stringing him up in a hangman's noose. But if the law found him guilty, he'd be for the drop, war or no war. But one thing, in particular, puzzled me. His mother had died in 1934. Why wait five years to take his revenge? Why this Christmas? It didn't make sense.

Caldwell and Miss Makepiece were the only two, apart from the boy, who admitted having left their rooms that night. Miss Makepiece said that, shortly after one o'clock, she had been woken by a call on her bedside telephone; Mickledore never took night calls and the extension was in her room. The call was from Bill Sowers, our Air Raid Warden, complaining that a strip of light was showing from one of the first-floor windows. Miss Makepiece had roused Caldwell and they had taken torches, unbolted a side door from the kitchen quarters, and had gone out together to identify the source of the light and check that the rest of the house was properly blacked out. Afterwards they had taken a nip of whisky from the decanter still in the great hall – it was a cold night to go traipsing round in dressing gowns – and had decided to play a game of chess. It seemed a bit odd to me, but they said they were by now thoroughly awake and disinclined for sleep. Both were experienced players and they welcomed the chance of a peaceful game. They couldn't remember which of them had suggested it but both agreed that the game had ended just before three when they had gone to their rooms for what remained of the night.

And here I thought I had them. I play a reasonable game myself so I asked them to sit at different ends of the room and write down as many of the moves as they could remember. It's strange, but I can recall some of that game to this day. Miss Makepiece was white and opened with pawn to king four. Caldwell responded by playing the Sicilian. After about ninety minutes, white managed to queen a pawn and black resigned. They were able to remember a remarkable number of moves and I was forced to accept that the game had been played. Caldwell had nerve. But had he nerve enough to play a complicated game of chess while his victim, still warm, lay murdered upstairs?

And that call from Bill Sowers was genuine, too. I had been with him when he made it from the village call box. We had come out of church together after midnight service and had immediately seen the offending light, as had most of the congregation. And Bill, always punctilious, had looked at his watch. His call to the Manor had been made at six minutes past one.

It was four thirty before I finally left the manor to report to the Chief Constable. Those were the days of the old-fashioned chiefs; none of your university special entrants or Police College intellectuals. I loved old Colonel Wallford. My own father had been killed at Ypres and I suppose he was some kind of substitute. He didn't start talking about the murder until his wife had settled me in front of their roaring fire with tea and a hefty slice of her homemade Christmas cake. He listened in silence to my account, then said:

'I've had Major Turville on the telephone. Perfectly

proper. What you'd expect from a gentleman. He thinks he ought not to sit on the Bench until this business is cleared up. Must say I agree with him.'

'Yes, Sir.'

'What's odd, although I didn't say so to him, is what he and Mrs Turville are doing at the manor. Hardly the sort of Christmas invitation you'd expect them to accept. Mickledore insisted on taking the place away from them complete, lock, stock and barrel, cheated them on the price if rumour's correct, and they choose to spend Christmas under his roof. Damned odd. And then there's the curious reaction of Mrs Turville. You still haven't had a chance to question her or search the room?'

'She let me in after Doc McKay had examined her. She was upset, naturally enough, but perfectly calm. All she could tell me was that she'd gone to sleep shortly after listening to the Dvořák String Quartet at ten fifty-five – they had twin beds – and didn't stir until her husband woke her with news of the murder.'

'Which promptly threw her into a state of shock. Not very likely, not with Mary Turville. Ever see her in the hunting field?'

'No, Sir.'

'She was younger then, of course. A different world. But Mrs Turville's not the kind to be thrown into shock by a body she didn't see.'

I said nothing. But I reckon he guessed my thoughts.

She could have seen it; been the first person to see it; seen it at that moment when it ceased to be Mickledore and became a body. The Chief went on:

'And that secretary cum housekeeper. Why does she stay? Rumour has it that he treats her like a slave.'

'I doubt that, Sir. She's too useful. It can't be easy to find a first-class secretary who'll also run your house.'

'Even so, it can't be an agreeable job.'

'She was quite frank about it. She has an invalid mother. Mickledore pays the nursing-home fees.'

'And a good salary in addition, no doubt.'

It was odd, I thought, how we were speaking of him in the present tense.

'And Gloria Belsize. What attracts her to the manor?'

I knew the answer to that one; it was to be found in a Christmas stocking. Last year, a diamond bracelet. This year an emerald clasp. Her story was that she had rushed impulsively into Mickledore's room to thank him for it and had found him dead. The Chief cut me another wedge of cake:

'That light we all saw after church. Anyone admit to that bit of carelessness?'

'It came from the back bathroom on the first floor. Only Charles Mickledore admits to visiting it in the night. He says he could have pulled back the curtain to look out over the fields, but he isn't sure.'

'Odd thing to be vague about. Still, it was Christmas

Eve. Excitement. A strange house. This Father Christmas nonsense of Mickledore's. You say that the boy was the only one to see him.'

'The only one to admit it.'

'Then he's a vital witness. Did he recognise his uncle?'

'Not definitely, Sir. But he says it never occurred to him that it wasn't Mickledore. And then there's the fact that he was given the present intended for Caldwell. Miss Makepiece says that only the boy, Caldwell and herself knew about the change of rooms.'

'Which suggests that Santa Claus didn't know, whoever he was. Or we are intended to believe just that?'

I said, 'What I can't understand is why the gun wasn't left by the body or replaced in the drawer. Why take it away and hide it?'

'Probably to cast doubt on whether it really is the weapon. We can't prove that until we find it. There are plenty of old service revolvers still around from the last war. Come to that, Saunders still has his uncle's. He mentioned it to me last month when we were discussing civilian defence. I'd forgotten that. Saunders has a revolver!'

'Not now, he hasn't, Sir. That's one thing I asked him when I went to question him and his wife about the cracker. He said he got rid of the weapon after his daughter was killed.'

'Did he say why?'

'Because he was afraid that the temptation to shoot Mickledore might get too much for him.'

'That's candid enough. What did he do with it?'

'Threw it in Potter's Pool, Sir.'

'Where it's now well down in the mud. Very convenient. No one has ever dredged anything from Potter's Pool. Still, you'd better try. We need that gun wherever it came from.'

I hadn't enjoyed my interview with the Saunderses. All the village respected Will and Edna; a decent, hardworking couple who had doted on their only daughter. We had been pretty friendly, but I knew that he and his wife resented the fact that we hadn't caught the hit-and-run driver of the Daimler that knocked down and killed their Dorothy. It wasn't for lack of trying. We knew, and they knew, that Mickledore was the suspect. He was the only owner of a Daimler in the neighbourhood and the accident had happened in the narrow lane from the manor. But there had been no identifiable damage to his car and Poole had been ready to swear that it had never left the garage. We couldn't arrest him on unsupported suspicion.

So I had to handle the interview with tact. They were just back from church when I arrived. We settled down in their neat sitting room and Mrs Saunders made up the fire. But they didn't offer me a drink as they once would have done, and I knew that they would be glad to see the back of me. And there was something else I knew. The murder of Mickledore wasn't news to them. They were on the telephone – Saunders ran the one village taxi – and I guessed that someone from the manor had rung with a warning. And I thought I knew who. Miss Makepiece and Edna Saunders were old college friends.

They denied any knowledge of the Christmas cracker or its message. After Mrs Saunders had returned from the carol singing they had spent the evening by the fire listening to the wireless. The news at nine o'clock, *Robinson Crusoe* at nine fifteen and 'The Crime Wave at Blandings' at ten. Mrs Saunders had particularly wanted to hear the Wodehouse play, as the actors Gladys Young and Carleton Hobbs were particular favourites.

They were able to tell me what had been on the nine o'clock news; the awards to officers and men of the submarine *Ursula*, the big IRA raid in Dublin, the Pope's Christmas message. I led them on gently to the crucial time. They said that they had listened to the Solemn Midnight Mass from Downside which had ended at twelve forty-five and had then gone to their bed. They were even able to describe the music. But that didn't mean that both of them had been listening. It hadn't taken more than one hand to put that bullet into Mickledore.

I wrenched my mind back to the present. The Chief was saying:

'It looks as if the cracker must have been brought

into the house by one of the carol singers. But I suppose it's not impossible for one of the house party to have planted it.'

'Only those who were near the door.'

'But if one or both of the Saunderses shot Mickledore they must have had an accomplice. They couldn't have known where to find the cracker. And they couldn't have got in unless the door was opened for them.'

'The back door was unbolted, Sir, while Caldwell and Miss Makepiece checked the lights. That was at about ten past one.'

'But the murderer couldn't have depended on that. There was no difficulty in getting into Mickledore's bedroom, of course. I respect his refusal to lock his door. And the obvious time for the murder was while he was delivering the presents. They all knew that his room would be empty. The murderer sneaks in, takes the gun and hides – where?'

'There's a large clothes closet, Sir.'

'Very convenient. And so was this game of hunt the hare. It gave the murderer the chance to steal the cracker, check on the gun, select a knife. He could safely be seen anywhere, even in another person's bedroom. Silly kind of game, though, for grown men. Who suggested it?'

'Mickledore. It's part of his ritual family Christmas.'

'Then the murderer could rely on its being played.

All he had to do was conceal the knife and cracker on his person until he could hide them in his room.'

'Not easy for Miss Belsize, Sir. She was wearing a slinky evening dress. And somehow I can't picture her scampering about in the kitchen.'

'Don't exclude her, John. If that will you found in the study still stands, she inherits £20,000. And so does Miss Makepiece. And Poole gets £10,000 you said. Men and women have killed for far less. Ah well, you'd better get back to it I suppose. We must find that gun.'

We were to find it all right. But more surprisingly and dramatically than either of us could have dreamed.

There are more agreeable ways of spending Christmas Day than being interrogated by the police, particularly by Inspector Pottinger with his dogged, impassive persistence, his accusing eyes. With the impulsive chivalry of the young, I had decided to protect Mrs Turville. I lied about seeing her and her husband in the night. I was deliberately vague when I described the visit of Santa Claus. I wasn't sure how far I managed to deceive Pottinger, but lying takes practice. I was to get better at it by the end of the case.

The questioning was ceaseless. Henry was even summoned to the study in the middle of Christmas dinner. It was an uncomfortable meal. Mrs Banting had already put the huge turkey in the oven when the murder was discovered and there was a general feeling that, having been cooked, it might as well be eaten. But Henry said firmly that the combination of Christmas pudding and violent death would be intolerably indigestible; the pudding would keep until next year. So we ate mince pies instead. I had the healthy appetite of youth and was embarrassingly aware that I was eating with undisguised enjoyment while the adults toyed with their lukewarm turkey and shredded Brussels sprouts.

Afterwards Poole served coffee in the hall and we listened in silence to the three o'clock King's broadcast. Nineteen thirty-nine was the occasion on which he finished with the quotation about the man standing at the gate of the year and asking for a light to guide him into the unknown. I have heard it many times since, but it has never sounded so poignant as it did spoken in the King's slow and careful voice on that Christmas of 1939.

It was a relief to us all when, at four thirty, Inspector Pottinger left the manor, leaving his Sergeant to continue the search for the gun. Poole, bringing in the tea, told us that the Inspector had gone to report to the Chief Constable; Poole had his own mysterious ways of discovering what the police were up to.

But we were not left in peace for long. Just before seven the Inspector returned. His imperious knock on the front door, clearly heard in the hall, was like the knock of doom. Poole showed him in with his usual insolent formality, and I watched the eyes of my companions turn to him with a mixture of apprehension and enquiry. The drinks tray had been brought in early and Gloria was noisily mixing cocktails for herself and Henry. But she must have been drinking earlier; even my inexperienced eyes could see that she was half-drunk. Before the Inspector could say more than a stolid 'Good evening' she swayed up to him glass in hand.

'Here comes our village Poirot with his little grey cells clicking away. But no handcuffs. Haven't you come to arrest poor little Gloria?'

Henry went quietly up to her. I heard him whisper urgently. But she laughed and advanced to the Christmas tree. Suddenly she began pulling off the decorations and throwing them wildly over him. A strand of tinsel caught on the Turville Grace, but Mrs Turville seemed not to care. Gloria began chanting.

'Time for pressies, everyone. We always have pressies off the tree at seven. Mustn't break with tradition. Victor wouldn't like it. One for you, Poole, and one for Mrs Banting. Catch!'

She tore the parcels from the tree and tossed them to Poole. He said an expressionless 'Thank you, Miss' and placed them on a side table. Henry moved forward and caught hold of her arm. But she wrenched herself free and seized another present from the tree.

'It's for you, darling. Henry, written in Victor's own hand.'

Henry's voice was like ice. I had never heard him speak in that tone before.

'Leave it. This isn't the time for presents. I'll take it home with me.'

'Don't be a spoilsport, darling! You want to see your pressie. Let Gloria open it for you.'

There was one of those moments of absolute silence which seem in retrospect so portentous. Perhaps I only now imagine, forty-four years later, that the whole room froze and watched breathless as she tore off the gaudy Christmas paper. Inside was a further wrapping of red and yellow crêpe; surely the paper from the Christmas cracker? This was wrapped round a couple of large linen handkerchiefs. But that wasn't all. Gloria unfolded them, gasped and let out a shrill scream. Her shaking hands parted. And the revolver, found at last, fell with a dull thud at Pottinger's feet.

After the discovery of the gun the atmosphere subtly changed. Before then we had comforted ourselves with the theory, which we all strenuously promoted, that a stranger had gained access to the manor by the unbolted side door while Henry and Miss Makepiece were checking the windows. He had discovered the cracker while searching the study and had stabbed the message to the body as a bizarre gesture of contempt.

Now it was less easy to believe that the killer came from outside. We stopped discussing the murder, afraid of what we might say or suggest, wary of each other's eyes. Mrs Turville, who looked suddenly like a very old woman, tried to reassure and comfort me. Relishing my shameful excitement in the face of murder, which has never left me, I was glad she didn't know how little I needed or deserved her kindness. The police questioning went on, more rigorous, more insistent. By the time Inspector Pottinger left we were all exhausted and glad of an excuse to seek an early bed.

It was ten o'clock when I heard a knock at my door. My heart thudded; I slipped out of bed and whispered, 'Who is it?' There was a second more insistent knock. Cautiously I opened the door. Gloria sidled in, trembling with fear and with cold.

'Charles, darling, could you bear to sleep in my room? There's a big armchair, and you could bring your eiderdown. I'm too terrified to be alone.'

'Can't you lock the door?'

'There isn't a lock. And I daren't take my sleeping pill in case he comes when I'm unconscious.'

'Who comes?'

'The murderer, of course.'

What sixteen year old could resist that appeal to chivalry? Flattered to be asked, and not sorry to have company, I pattered along the corridor behind her. We pushed the heavy armchair against the door and I settled down in reasonable comfort. It was curiously cosy in her bedroom with the pool of light from the bedside lamp shining on her fair hair. We spoke in whispers like conspirators.

'They think Victor was doped with my sleeping pills and then shot while he slept. Pottinger keeps on asking me if any are missing. How can I tell? My Mayfair doctor lets me have what I ask. I've got a whole bottle here in my bedside drawer. Anyone could have helped himself. I don't count them.'

I said, 'But wouldn't he taste the pills?'

'Not in his whisky. I never can.'

She propped herself on her elbow and leaned towards me.

'Have you thought about Poole? Poole could have done it. He knows that Victor killed the Saunders child. He lied about the Daimler never leaving the garage. He had to. Victor had something on him.'

'Had what on him?'

'He's been in prison for assaulting small girls. He wouldn't last long in the village if that came out. And it's very convenient for him that Victor died when he did. He was thinking of changing his will. That's why you're here. If he liked you, he was thinking of making you his heir and cutting the rest of us out.'

It had been convenient for her, too, I thought, that my

uncle had died when he had. I whispered:

'How do you know about the will?'

'Victor told me. He liked tormenting me. He could be terribly cruel. People say that he drove his wife to suicide.'

Gloria had swallowed her sleeping pill by now and her voice was becoming blurred. I had to strain to hear her.

'And then there's the Turvilles.'

'What about the Turvilles?'

I realised that my voice had betrayed me. She laughed sleepily.

'You like her, don't you? Everyone does. The perfect lady. Not like little Gloria. Must protect the dear Turvilles. But they're up to something. Their door was ajar. The deaf don't realise how loudly they whisper. He was saying, "We have to go through with it, darling. We've spent the money and we've planned it so carefully . . . So carefully." ' Gloria's voice faded into silence.

Spent what money and for what? I wondered as I lay there listening to Gloria's low guttural breathing. Wakeful, I relived all the events of that extraordinary Christmas. My arrival at Marston station, the silent drive through the darkening village; the school with the Christmas chains of coloured paper gleaming against the windows. The first sight of my uncle's dark judgemental face. The carol singers creeping out under the blackout curtain. The game of hunt the hare. The silent figure of Santa Claus at the foot of my bed. Myself, standing by Victor's bed and noting every detail of that grotesquely clad, unreal corpse. Doctor McKay leaving Mrs Turville's room with his old-fashioned Gladstone bag. The strand of tinsel thrown by Gloria over the Turville Grace. The gun thudding at Pottinger's feet.

The varied images flashed upon my inner eye like camera shots. And suddenly, the confused medley of sights and sounds fused into a coherent picture. Before I fell asleep I knew what I must do. Tomorrow I would first speak to Inspector Pottinger. And then I would confront the murderer.

I saw Inspector Pottinger first and told him what I had to tell. Then I sought out Henry. He was in the great hall with the Turvilles and I asked if I might speak to him alone. Tactful as ever they got up and silently left. I said:

'I know it was you.'

That sixteen-year-old boy is a stranger to me now and memory is self-deluding. I couldn't, surely, have been so confident, so self-assured as I seem to recall. But there is no doubt about what I had to say. And I remember perfectly – how could I ever forget? – how he looked and the words he spoke to me.

He looked down at me calmly, unfrightened, a little sadly.

'Suppose you tell me how.'

'When Santa Claus slipped your present into my

stocking he was wearing a white glove. The murderer would have needed to wear gloves to avoid fingerprints. But the hands of the corpse were bare and I could see no gloves by the bed.'

'And you kept this vital piece of evidence from the police?'

'I wanted to protect the Turvilles. I saw them creeping about suspiciously in the night. He was carrying a rolled towel. I thought it concealed the gun.'

'And how did you imagine they got rid of it? Pottinger searched our rooms.'

'Mrs Turville feigned illness. I thought she gave the gun to Dr McKay after he'd seen her. He could have taken it away in his Gladstone bag.'

'But when the gun was found, you realised that your theory was wrong. The Turvilles were innocent.'

'And last night I guessed the truth. Dr McKay did take something away in his bag: the Turville Grace. That's what they were doing; substituting a fake statue for the one they believe will protect their son. They were desperate to regain it now that he's gone to war.'

'So now you pick on me as suspect number one. Am I also supposed to have fabricated and planted the cracker?'

'No. You and I stood together during the carol singing. You were never near the door. I think you used it to complicate the crime – that's why you suggested keeping it – but it was Mrs Saunders who made it. She could have taken some of the crêpe paper her schoolchildren were provided with to make their Christmas decorations. I noticed, too, that the verse was written by someone who punctuated correctly as if by instinct. And it didn't threaten death. All they wanted was to harass Victor, to spoil his Christmas. It was a small, pathetic revenge for the death of their daughter.'

'Well, go on. So far it's remarkably convincing.'

'You took the cracker and the kitchen knife and stole some of Gloria's sleeping pills while we were playing hunt the hare. The game is traditional at the manor. You could rely on its being played. And it was you who asked for a change of room. You wanted to be close to my uncle and to have me further away in case I heard the shot. The Turvilles are deaf and Gloria takes sleeping pills. My young ears were the danger. But even I couldn't hear a shot in that heavily curtained bed. You can't really be claustrophobic, can you? The RAF wouldn't have accepted you if you were.'

He looked down on me, his pale handsome face still calm, still unfrightened. And I realised again that he must have been Santa Claus. No one else in the house could match my uncle's height.

When he spoke, his voice was ironic, almost amused.

'Don't stop now. Aren't you getting to the exciting part?'

'You slipped the sleeping pills in Victor's whisky while you were drinking together or, perhaps, later while he was in the bathroom. Then you took his gun and shot him while he lay drugged and undressed on his bed, probably between twelve fifteen and twelve thirty. Promptly at one o'clock you took the part of Santa Claus, being careful to leave your present in my stocking. Then you dressed the corpse in the robes and drove in the knife through the menacing cracker rhyme. It was you who pulled aside that curtain in the bathroom knowing that it would bring an immediate call. If Miss Makepiece hadn't woken you – but you were the natural choice – you would have pretended to hear her prowling about outside. There was no difficulty in persuading her to play chess with you and thus innocently provide you with that vital alibi for the hours after one o'clock.'

He said calmly, 'Congratulations. You should write detective stories. Is there anything you don't know?'

'Yes. What you did with the white gloves and the death's head charm from the cracker.'

He looked at me with a half-smile, then bent and rummaged among the cotton-wool snowballs round the foot of the Christmas tree. He brought one out, a rolled white ball with strands of cotton wool and tinsel still adhering to it. Deliberately he threw it into the fire. The flames licked at it, then blazed high.

'I've been waiting for the chance to do that. The fire

had died by midnight and ever since it was relit this room has been occupied.'

'And the charm?'

'Someone will break a tooth on it next Christmas. I took the cloth and greaseproof paper off the Christmas pudding and pressed it in among the sixpenny pieces. Even if it's found next year it will be too late to help Pottinger.'

'And, immediately after the shooting, you wrapped the gun in the crêpe paper and hid it in the Christmas tree present bearing your name. You would have taken it away with you when you left the manor if Gloria hadn't found it so dramatically. No wonder you tried to restrain her.'

He said, 'There's no witness to this conversation. I'm trusting you; but not perhaps as much as you suppose.'

I looked at him full in the face.

'I'm trusting you, too. Five minutes ago I asked to see Inspector Pottinger and told him that I'd remembered something vital. I said that, when Santa Claus slipped your present into my stocking, I distinctly saw the gold of his signet ring. Your fingers are much thicker than Victor's. You couldn't have forced on that ring. If I stick to my lie – and I shall – they won't dare arrest you.'

He didn't thank me. I didn't say anything. I cried out: 'But why? And why now, this Christmas?'

'Because he murdered my mother. Oh, not in any way I can prove. But she killed herself after only two years of marriage to him. I always meant to destroy him, but the years pass and the will atrophies. And then came the war. This phoney war won't last much longer and there will be nothing phoney about the killing once it begins in earnest. I'll be shooting down young pilots, decent ordinary Germans with whom I've no quarrel. It has to be done. They'll do it to me if they can. But it will be more tolerable now that I've killed the one man who did deserve it. I've kept faith with her. If I have to go, I'll go more easily.'

I picture that blazing Spitfire spiralling into the Channel and I wonder if he did.

I've posted my account of the Marston Turville murder to Charles Mickledore, but God knows why he wanted it. It was hardly my most successful case; I never made an arrest and the mystery remains to this day. Once the boy recalled seeing that ring on his uncle's finger my case against Caldwell collapsed. The medical evidence showed that Mickledore was dead before three o'clock when Caldwell and Miss Makepiece finished their game of chess. Caldwell couldn't have shot him and done all that was necessary in those few minutes between the delivery of the presents and the warden's telephone call.

His alibi held.

The Turvilles were killed by a V2 rocket while on a day trip to London. Well, that's how they would have wanted to go, quickly and together. But there are Turvilles still at the manor. Their son survived the war and bought back his ancestral home. I wonder if his grandchildren frighten themselves on Christmas Eve with tales of the murder of Santa Claus.

Neither Poole nor Miss Belsize benefited long from their legacies. She bought herself a Bentley and killed herself in it, driving while drunk. He purchased a house in the village and played the gentleman. But within a year he was up to his old tricks with small girls. I was actually on my way to arrest him when he hanged himself in his garage, choked to death on the end of a washing line. The public hangman would have made a neater job of it.

I sometimes wonder if young Charles Mickledore lied about seeing that ring. Now that we're in touch, I'm tempted to ask him. But it was over forty years ago; an old crime, an old story. And if Henry Caldwell did owe a debt to society, he paid it at last and in full.

The Girl Who Loved Graveyards

She couldn't remember anything about that day in the hot August of 1956 when they took her to live with her Aunt Gladys and Uncle Gordon in the small house in East London, at 49 Alma Terrace. She knew that it was three days after her tenth birthday and that she was to be cared for by her only living relations now that her father and grandmother were dead, killed by influenza within a week of each other. But those were just facts someone, at some time, had told her briefly. She could remember nothing of her previous life. Those first ten years were a void, unsubstantial as a dream that had faded but that had left on her mind a scar of unarticulated childish anxiety and fear. For her, memory and childhood both began with that moment when, waking in the small, unfamiliar bedroom with the kitten, Blackie, still curled up asleep on a towel at the foot of her bed, she had walked barefoot to the window and drawn back the curtain. And there, stretched beneath her, lay the cemetery, luminous and mysterious in the early morning light, bounded by iron railings and separated from the rear of Alma Terrace only by a narrow path. It was to be another warm day, and over the serried rows of headstones lay a thin haze pierced by the occasional obelisk and by the wing tips of marble angels whose disembodied heads seemed to be floating on particles of shimmering light. And as she watched, motionless in an absorbed enchantment, the mist began to rise and the whole cemetery was revealed to her, a miracle of stone and marble, bright grass and summer-laden trees, flower-bedecked graves and intersecting paths stretching as far as the eye could see. In the distance she could just make out the spire of a Victorian chapel, gleaming like the spire of some magical castle in a long-forgotten fairy tale. In those moments of growing wonder she found herself shivering with delight, an emotion so rare that it stole through her thin body like a pain. And it was then, on the first morning of her new life, with the past a void and the future unknown and frightening, that she made the cemetery her own. Throughout her childhood and youth it was to remain a place of delight and mystery, her refuge and her solace.

It was a childhood without love, almost without affection. Her uncle Gordon was her father's elder half-brother; that too she had been told. He and her aunt weren't really her relations. Their small capacity for love was expended on each other, and even here it was less a positive emotion than a pact of mutual support and comfort against the threatening world that lay outside the trim curtains of their small, claustrophobic sitting room.

But they cared for her as dutifully as she cared for the cat Blackie. It was a fiction in the household that she adored Blackie, her own cat, brought with her when she arrived, her one link with the past, almost her only possession. Only she knew that she disliked and feared him. But she brushed and fed him with conscientious care as she did everything, and in return he gave her a slavish allegiance, hardly ever leaving her side, slinking through the cemetery at her heels and turning back only when they reached the main gate. But he wasn't her friend. He didn't love her and he knew she didn't love him. He was a fellow conspirator, gazing at her through slits of azure light, relishing some secret knowledge that was her knowledge too. He ate voraciously, yet he never grew fat. Instead his sleek black body lengthened until – stretched in the sunlight along her windowsill, his sharp nose turned always to the cemetery – he looked as sinister and unnatural as a furred reptile.

It was lucky for her that there was a side gate to the cemetery from Alma Terrace and that she could take a short cut to and from school across the graveyard, avoiding the dangers of the main road. On her first morning her uncle had said doubtfully, 'I suppose it's all right. But it seems wrong, somehow, a child walking every day through rows of the dead.'

Her aunt had replied: 'The dead can't rise from their graves. They lie quiet. She's safe enough from the dead.'

Her voice had been unnaturally gruff and loud. The words had sounded like an assertion, almost a defiance. But the child knew her aunt was right. She did feel safe with the dead – safe and at home. The years in Alma Terrace slipped by, as bland and dull as her aunt's blancmange, a sensation rather than a taste. Was she happy? That was a question it had never occurred to her to ask. She wasn't unpopular at school, being neither pretty nor intelligent enough to provoke much interest either from the children or the staff; an ordinary child, unusual only in that she was an orphan, but unable to capitalise even on that sentimental advantage. Perhaps she might have found friends, quiet, unenterprising children like her, who would respond to her unthreatening mediocrity, but something about her repelled their timid advances: her self-sufficiency, the bland, uncaring gaze, the refusal to give anything of herself even in casual friendship. She didn't need friends. She had the graveyard and its occupants.

She had her favourites. She knew them all – when they had died, how old they had been, sometimes how they had died. She knew their names and learned their memorials by heart. They were more real to her than the living, those rows of dearly loved wives and mothers, respected tradesmen, lamented fathers, deeply mourned children.

The new graves hardly ever interested her, although

she would watch the funerals from a distance and creep up later to read the mourning cards. What she liked best were the old, neglected oblongs of mounded earth or chipped stones, the tilted crosses, the carved words almost erased by time. It was around the names of the long dead that she wove her childish fantasies.

Even the seasons of the year she experienced in and through the cemetery. The gold and purple spears of the first crocuses thrusting through the hard earth. April with its tossing daffodils. The whole graveyard *en fête* in yellow and white, as mourners dressed the graves for Easter. The smell of mown grass and the earthy tang of high summer, as if the dead were breathing the flower-scented air and exuding their own mysterious perfume. The glare of sunlight on stone and marble as the old women in their stained cotton dresses shuffled with their vases to fill them at the tap behind the chapel. Seeing the cemetery transformed by the first snow of winter, the marble angels grotesque in their high bonnets of glistening white. Watching at her window for the thaw, hoping to catch that moment when the edifice would slip and the shrouded shapes become themselves again.

Only once had she asked about her father, and then she had known, as children do, that this was a subject which, for some mysterious adult reason, it was better not to talk about. She had been sitting at the kitchen table with her homework while her aunt was busy cooking supper. Looking up from her history book, she asked: 'Where is Daddy buried?'

The frying pan clattered against the stove. The cooking fork dropped from her aunt's hand. It took her a long time to pick it up, wash it, clean the grease from the floor. The child asked once again: 'Where is Daddy buried?'

'Up north. At Creedon, outside Nottingham, with your mum and gran. Where else?'

'Can I go there? Can I visit him?'

'When you're older, maybe. No sense, is there, hanging about graves? The dead aren't there.'

'Who looks after them?'

'The graves? The cemetery people. Now get on with your homework.' She hadn't asked about her mother, the mother who died when she was born. That desertion had always seemed to her wilful, a source of secret guilt. 'You killed your mother.' Someone sometime had spoken those words to her, had laid on her that burden. She wouldn't let herself think about her mother. But she knew that her father had stayed with her, had loved her, hadn't wanted to die and leave her. Someday, secretly, she would find his grave. She would visit it, not once, but every week. She would tend it and plant flowers on it and clip the grass as the old ladies did in the cemetery. And if there wasn't a stone, she would pay for one, bearing his name and an epitaph she would choose. She would have to wait until she was older, until she could leave school and go to work and save enough money. But one day she would find her father. She would have a grave of her own to visit and tend. There was a debt of love to be paid.

Four years after her arrival in Alma Terrace, her aunt's only brother came to visit from Australia. Physically, he and his sister were alike, the same stolid, short-legged bodies, the same small eyes set in square, pudgy faces. But Uncle Ned had a brash assurance, a cheerful geniality that was so alien to his sister's unconfident reserve that it was hard to believe they were siblings. For two weeks he dominated the little house with his strident, alien voice and assertive masculinity. There were unfamiliar treats, dinners in the West End, a show at Earls Court. He was kind to the child, tipping her lavishly, even walking through the cemetery with her one morning on his way to buy his racing paper. And it was that evening, coming silently down the stairs to supper, that she overheard disjointed scraps of conversation, adult talk, incomprehensible at the time but taken into her mind and stored there.

First the harsh boom of her uncle's voice: 'We were looking at this gravestone together, see. "Beloved husband and father. Taken from us suddenly on March 14th 1892." Something like that. Marble chips, cracked urn, bloody great angel pointing upward. You know the kind of thing. Then the kid turned to me. "Daddy's death was sudden too." That's what she said. Came out with it cool as you please. Now, what in God's name made her say that? It gave me a turn, I can tell you. I didn't know where to put my face. And what a place to choose, the bloody cemetery. I'll say one thing for coming out to St Kilda – you'll get a better view. I can promise you that.'

Creeping closer, she strained her ears vainly to catch the indistinct mutter of her aunt's reply. Then came her uncle's voice again:

'That old bitch never forgave him for getting Helen pregnant.

'No one was good enough for her precious only daughter. And then when Helen died having the kid, she blamed him for that too. Poor sod. Sidney bought a packet of trouble when he set eyes on that girl.'

Again the murmur of indistinguishable voices, the sound of her aunt's footsteps moving from table to stove, the scrape of a chair. Then her uncle Ned's voice again:

'Funny kid, isn't she? Old-fashioned. Morbid, you might say. Seems to live in that boneyard, she and that damned cat. And the spitting image of her dad.

'It gave me a turn, I can tell you. Looking at me with his eyes and then coming out with it: "Daddy's death was sudden too." I'll say it was! Helps having such an ordinary name, I suppose. People don't catch on. How long ago? Four years? It seems longer.'

Only one part of this half-heard, incomprehensible conversation had disturbed her. Uncle Ned was trying to persuade them to join him in Australia. She might be taken away from Alma Terrace, might never see the cemetery again, might have to wait for years before she could save enough money to return to England and find her father's grave. And how could she visit it regularly, how could she tend and care for it, from the other side of the world? After Uncle Ned's visit ended, it was months before she could see one of his rare letters with the Australian stamp drop through the letterbox without feeling the cold clutch of fear at her heart.

She needn't have worried. It was October of 1966 before they left England, and they went alone. When they broke the news to her one Sunday morning at breakfast, it was apparent that they had never even considered taking her with them. Dutiful as ever, they had waited to make their decision until she had left school and was earning her living as a shorthand typist with a local firm of estate agents. Her future was assured. They had done all that conscience required of them. Hesitant and a little shamefaced, they justified their decision as if they believed that it was important to her. Her aunt's arthritis was increasingly troublesome; they longed for the sun; Uncle Ned was their only close relation and none of them was getting any younger. Their plan, over which they had agonised for months in whispers behind closed doors, was to visit St Kilda for six months and then, if they liked Australia, to apply to emigrate. The house in Alma Terrace was to be sold to pay the air fare. It was already on the market. But they had made provision for her. When they told her what had been arranged, she had to bend her face low over her plate lest the flood of joy be too apparent. Mrs Morgan, three doors down, would be glad to take her as a lodger if she didn't mind having the small bedroom at the back overlooking the cemetery. In the surging tumult of relief she hardly heard her aunt's next words. Everyone knew how Mrs Morgan was about cats. Blackie would have to be put to sleep.

She was to move into 43 Alma Terrace on the afternoon of the day on which her aunt and uncle flew from Heathrow. Her two cases, holding all that she possessed in the world, were already packed. In her handbag she carefully stowed the meagre official confirmations of her existence: her birth certificate, her medical card, her Post Office book showing the £103 painstakingly saved towards the cost of her father's memorial. The next day, she would begin her search. But first she took Blackie to the veterinarian to be destroyed. She had made a cat box and sat patiently in the waiting room with the box at her feet. The cat made no sound, and this patient resignation touched her, evoking for the first time a spasm of pity and affection. But there was nothing she could do to save him. They both knew it. But then it seemed he had always known what she was thinking, what was past and what was to come. There was something they shared, some knowledge, some common experience she couldn't remember and he couldn't express. Now, with his destruction, even that tenuous link with her first ten years would go forever.

When it was her turn to go into the surgery she said, 'I want him put to sleep.'

The veterinarian passed his strong, experienced hands over the sleek fur. 'Are you sure? He seems healthy still. He's old, of course, but in remarkably good condition.'

'I'm sure. I want him put to sleep.'

And she left him there without a glance or another word. She had thought that she would be glad to be free of the pretence of loving him, free of those slitted, accusing eyes. But as she walked back to Alma Terrace she found herself crying: tears, unbidden and unstoppable, ran like rain down her face.

There was no difficulty in getting a week's leave from her job; she had been husbanding her holiday entitlement. Her work, as always, was up to date. She had calculated how much money she would need for her train and bus fares and for a week's stay in modest hotels. Her plans had been made. They had been made for years. She would begin her search with the address on her birth certificate – Cranstoun House, Creedon, Nottingham, the house where she was born. The present owners might remember her father and her. If not, there would be neighbours or older inhabitants of the village who would be able to recall her father's death, where he was buried. If that failed, she would try the local undertakers. It was, after all, only ten years ago. Someone would remember. Somewhere in Nottingham there would be a record of burials. She told Mrs Morgan that she was taking a week's holiday to visit her father's old home, packed a holdall with necessities and next morning caught the earliest possible train to Nottingham.

It was during the bus ride from Nottingham to Creedon that she felt the first stirrings of anxiety and mistrust. Until then she had travelled in calm confidence, but strangely without excitement, as if this long-planned journey were as natural and inevitable as her daily walk to work, an inescapable pilgrimage ordained from that moment when a barefoot child in her white nightdress drew back her bedroom curtains and saw her kingdom spread beneath her. But now her mood changed. As the bus lurched through the suburbs she found herself shifting in her seat as if mental unease were provoking physical discomfort. She had expected green countryside, small churches guarding neat, domestic graveyards patterned with yew trees. These were graveyards she had visited on holidays, had loved almost as much as she loved the one she had made her own. Surely it was in such bird-loud, sanctified peace that her father lay. But Nottingham had spread out during the past ten years, and Creedon was now little more than an urban village separated from the city by a ribbon development of brash new houses, petrol stations and parades of shops. Nothing was familiar, and yet she knew that she had travelled this road before and travelled it in anxiety and pain. When, thirty minutes later, the bus stopped at its terminus at Creedon, she knew at once where she was. The Dog and Whistle still stood at one corner of the dusty, litter-strewn village green with the same bus shelter outside it. And at the sight of its graffiti-scrawled walls, memory returned as if nothing had ever been forgotten. Here her father used to leave her when he brought her to pay her regular Sunday visits to her grandmother. Here her grandmother's elderly cook would be waiting for her. Here she would look back for a final wave and see her father patiently waiting for the bus to begin its return journey. Here she would be brought at six thirty, when he arrived to collect her. Cranstoun House was where her grandmother lived. She herself had been born there but it had never been her home.

She had no need to ask her way to the house. And

when, five minutes later, she stood gazing up at it in appalled fascination, no need to read the name painted on the shabby, padlocked gate. It was a square building of dark brick standing in incongruous and spurious grandeur at the end of a country lane. It was smaller than she remembered, but it was still a dreadful house. How could she ever have forgotten those ornate overhanging gables, the high-pitched roof, the secretive oriel windows, the single forbidding turret at the east end? There was an estate agent's board wired to the gate; the house itself was empty. The paint on the front door was peeling, the lawns were overgrown, the boughs of the rhododendron bushes were broken and the gravel path was studded with weeds. There was no one here who could help her to find her father's grave. But she knew that she had to visit, had to make herself pass again through that intimidating front door. There was something the house knew and had to tell her, something Blackie had known. She couldn't escape her next step. She must find the estate agent's office and get a permit to view.

She had missed the returning bus, and by the time the next one had reached Nottingham, it was after three. Although she had eaten nothing since her early breakfast, she was too driven now to be aware of hunger. But she knew that it would be a long day and that she ought to eat. She turned into a coffee bar and had a toasted cheese sandwich and a mug of coffee, grudging the few minutes it took to gulp them down. The coffee was hot and almost tasteless, but she realised as the liquid stung her throat how much she had needed it.

The girl at the cash desk was able to direct her to the house agent's office, a ten-minute walk away. She was received by a sharp-featured young man in a pin-stripe suit who, after one practised glance at her old blue tweed coat, the cheap holdall and bag of synthetic leather, placed her precisely in his private category of client from whom little could be expected and to whom less needed to be given. But he found the particulars for her, and his curiosity sharpened as she merely glanced at them and then folded the paper away in her bag. Her request to view that afternoon was received, as she had expected, with politeness but without enthusiasm. But this was familiar territory and she knew why. The house was unoccupied. She would have to be escorted. There was nothing in her respectable drabness to suggest that she was a likely purchaser. And when he briefly excused himself to consult a colleague and returned to say that he would drive her to Creedon at once, she knew the probable reason for that too. The office wasn't busy and it was time that someone from the firm checked up on the property.

Neither of them spoke during the drive. When they reached Creedon and he turned down the lane to the house, the apprehension she had felt on her first visit returned, only it was deeper and stronger. Now it was more than the memory of an old wretchedness. This was childhood misery and fear relived, and intensified by a dreadful adult foreboding. The house agent parked his Morris on the grassy verge, and as she looked up at the blind windows she was seized by a spasm of terror so acute that momentarily she was unable to speak or move. She was aware of the man's holding open the door for her, of the smell of beer on his breath, of his face, uncomfortably close, bending on her a look of exasperated patience. She wanted to say that she had changed her mind, that the house was totally wrong for her, that there would be no point in viewing it, that she would wait for him in the car. But she willed herself to rise from the warm seat and scrambled out under his supercilious eyes. She waited in silence as he unlocked the padlock and swung open the gate.

They passed together between the neglected lawns and the spreading rhododendron bushes towards the front door. And suddenly the feet shuffling on the gravel beside her were different feet and she knew that she was walking with her father as she had walked in childhood. She had only to stretch out her hand to feel the grasp of his fingers. Her companion was saying something about the house but she didn't hear. The meaningless chatter faded and she heard a different voice, her father's voice, heard for the first time in over ten years:

'It won't be for always, darling. Just until I've found a job. And I'll visit you every Sunday for lunch. Afterwards we'll be able to go for a walk together, just the two of us. Grannie has promised that. And I'll buy you a kitten. I'm sure Grannie won't mind when she sees him. A black kitten. You've always wanted a black kitten. What shall we call him? Little Blackie? He'll remind you of me. And then when I've found a job, I'll be able to rent a little house and we'll be together again. I'll look after you, my darling. We'll look after each other.'

She dared not look up lest she see again those desperately pleading eyes begging her to understand, to make things easy for him, not to despise him. She knew now that she ought to have helped him, to have told him that she understood, that she didn't mind living with Grannie for a month or so, that everything would be all right. But she hadn't managed so adult a response. She remembered tears, desperate clinging to his coat, her grandmother's old cook, tight-lipped, pulling her away from him and bearing her up to bed. And the last memory was of watching him from her room above the porch, of his drooping, defeated figure making its way down the lane to the bus stop.

As they reached the front door she looked up. The window was still there. Of course it was. She knew every room in this dark house.

The garden was bathed in a mellow October sunlight, yet the hall struck cold and dim. The heavy mahogany staircase led up from gloom to a darkness which hung above them like a weight. The estate agent felt along the wall for the light switch. She didn't wait. She grasped again the huge brass doorknob that her childish fingers had hardly encompassed and moved unerringly into the drawing room. The smell of the room was different. Then there had been a scent of violets overlaid with furniture polish. Now the air smelled cold and musty. She stood in the darkness, shivering but perfectly calm. It seemed to her that she had passed through a barrier of fear as a tortured victim might pass through a pain barrier into a kind of peace. She felt a shoulder brush against her as the man went across to the window and swung open the heavy curtains.

He said, 'The last owners have left it partly furnished. Looks better that way. Easier to get offers if the place looks lived in.'

'Has there been an offer?'

'Not yet. It's not everyone's cup of tea. Bit on the large side for a modern family. Then too, there's the murder. Ten years ago, but people still talk. There've been four owners since, and none of them stayed long. It's bound to affect the price. No good thinking you can hush up murder.'

His voice was carefully nonchalant but his gaze

never left her face. Walking to the empty fire grate, he stretched one arm along the mantelpiece and followed her with his eyes as she moved trance-like about the room. She heard herself asking: 'What murder?'

'A sixty-four-year-old woman. Battered to death by her son-in-law. The old cook came in from the back kitchen and found him with the poker in his hand. Come to think of it, it could have been one like that.' He nodded at the collection of brass fire irons resting against the fender. He said, 'It happened right where you're standing now. She was sitting in that very chair.'

She said in a voice so strained and harsh that she hardly recognised it, 'It wasn't this chair. It was bigger. Her chair had an embroidered seat and back and there were armrests edged with crochet and the feet were like lions' claws.'

His gaze sharpened. Then he laughed warily. The watchful eyes grew puzzled, then the look changed into something else. Could it have been contempt?

'So you know about it. You're one of those.'

'One of those?'

'You aren't really in the market for a place. Couldn't afford one this size anyway. You just want a thrill, want to see where it happened. You get all sorts in this game and I can usually tell. I can give you all the gory details you're interested in. Not that there was much gore. The skull was smashed but most of the bleeding was internal. They say there was just a trickle falling down her forehead and dripping on to her hands.'

It came out so pat that she knew he had told it all before; he enjoyed telling it, this small recital of horror to titillate his clients and relieve the boredom of his day. She wished she weren't so cold. If only she could get warm again, her voice wouldn't sound so strange. She said through her dry lips, 'And the kitten. Tell me about the kitten.'

'Now, that was something! That was a touch of horror. The kitten was on her lap, licking up the blood. But then, you know, don't you. You've heard all about it."

'Yes,' she lied. 'I heard all about it.' But she had done more than that. She knew. She had seen it. She had been there.

And then the outline of the chair before her altered. An amorphous black shape swam before her eyes; then it took form and substance. Her grandmother was sitting there, squat as a toad, dressed in her Sunday black for morning service, gloved and hatted, prayer book in her lap. She saw again the glob of phlegm at the corner of the mouth, the thread of broken veins at the side of the sharp nose. The grandmother was waiting to inspect her grandchild before church, turning on her again that look of querulous discontent. The witch was sitting there. The witch who hated her and her Daddy, who had told her that he was useless and feckless and no better than her mother's murderer. The witch who was threatening to have Blackie put to sleep because he had torn her chair, because Daddy had given him to her. The witch who was planning to keep her from Daddy for ever. And then she saw something else. The poker was there too, just as she remembered it, the long rod of polished brass with its heavy knob.

She seized it now as she had seized it then, and with a scream of hatred and terror, brought it down on her grandmother's head. Again and again she struck, hearing the brass thudding against the leather, blow on splitting blow. And still she screamed. The room rang with the terror of it. But it was only when the frenzy passed and the dreadful noise stopped that she knew from the pain of her throat that the screaming had been hers.

She stood shaking, gasping for breath. Beads of sweat stood out on her forehead and she felt the stinging drops seeping into her eyes. Looking up, she was aware of the man's eyes, wide with terror, staring into hers, of a muttered curse, of footsteps running to the door. And then the poker slid from her moist hands and she heard it thud softly on the rug.

He had been right; there was no blood. Only the grotesque hat knocked forward over the dead face. But while she watched, a sluggish line of deep red rolled from under the brim, zigzagged down the forehead, trickled along the creases of the cheeks and began to drop steadily onto the gloved hands. And then she heard a soft mew. A ball of black fur crept from behind the chair and the ghost of Blackie, azure eyes frantic, leaped, as he had leaped ten years earlier, delicately into that unmoving lap. She looked at her hands. Where were the gloves, the white cotton gloves that the witch had always insisted must be worn to church? But these hands, no longer the hands of a nine-year-old child, were naked. And the chair was empty. There was nothing but the split leather, the burst of horsehair stuffing, a faint smell of violets fading on the quiet air.

She walked out the front door without closing it behind her as she had left it then. She walked as she had walked then, gloved and unsullied, down the gravel path between the rhododendrons, through the ironwork gate and up the lane towards the church. The bell had only just started ringing: she would be in good time. In the distance she had glimpsed her father climbing a stile from the water meadow into the lane. So he must have set out early after breakfast and had walked to Creedon. And why so early? Had he needed that long walk to settle something in his mind? Had it been a pathetic attempt to propitiate the witch by coming with them to church? Or – blessed thought – had he come to take her away, to see that her few belongings were packed and ready by the time the service was over? Yes, that was what she had thought at the time. She remembered it now, that fountain of hope soaring and dancing into glorious certainty. When she got home, all would be ready. They would stand there together and defy the witch, would tell her that they were leaving together, the two of them and Blackie, that she would never see them again. At the end of the road she looked back and saw for the last time the beloved ghost, crossing the lane to the house towards that fatally open door.

And after that? The vision was fading now. She could remember nothing of the service except a blaze of red and blue shifting like a kaleidoscope, then fusing into a stained-glass window, the Good Shepherd gathering a lamb to his bosom. And afterwards? Surely there had been strangers waiting on the porch, grave, concerned faces, whispers and sidelong glances, a woman in some kind of uniform, an official car. And after that, nothing. Memory was a blank. But now at last she knew where her father was buried. And she knew why she would never be able to visit him, never make that pious pilgrimage to the place where he lay because of her, the shameful place where she had put him. There could be no flowers, no obelisk, no loving message carved in marble for those who lay in quicklime behind a prison wall. And then, unbidden, came the final memory. She saw again the open church door, the congregation filing in, enquiring faces turning towards her as she arrived alone in the vestibule. She heard again that high, childish voice speaking the words that more than any others had slipped the rope of hemp over his shrouded head.

'Granny? She isn't very well. She told me to come on my own. No, there's nothing to worry about. She's quite all right. Daddy's with her.'

A Very Desirable Residence

During and after Harold Vinson's trial, at which I was a relatively unimportant prosecution witness, there was the usual uninformed, pointless and repetitive speculation about whether those of us who knew him would ever have guessed that he was a man capable of scheming to murder his wife. I was supposed to have known him better than most of the school staff, and my colleagues found it irritatingly self-righteous of me to be so very reluctant to be drawn into the general gossip about what, after all, was the school's major scandal in twenty years. 'You knew them both. You used to visit the house. You saw them together. Didn't you guess?' they insisted, obviously feeling that I had been in some way negligent, that I ought to have seen what was going on and prevented it. No, I never guessed; or, if I did, I guessed wrong. But they were perfectly right. I could have prevented it.

I first met Harold Vinson when I took up a post as junior art master at the comprehensive school where he taught mathematics to the senior forms. It wasn't too discouraging a place, as these teaching factories go. The school was centred on the old eighteenth-century grammar school, with some not-too-hideous modern additions, in a pleasant enough commuter town on the river about twenty miles south-east of London. It was a predominantly middle-class community, a little smug and culturally self-conscious, but hardly intellectually exciting. Still, it suited me well enough for a first post. I don't object to the middle class or their habitats; I'm middle class myself. And I knew that I was lucky to get the job. Mine is the usual story of an artist with sufficient talent but without enough respect for the fashionable idiocies of the contemporary artistic establishment to make a decent living. More dedicated men choose to live in cheap bedsitting rooms and keep on painting. I'm fussy about where and how I live so, for me, it was a diploma in the teaching of art and West Fairing Comprehensive.

It only took one evening in Vinson's home for me to realise that he was a sadist. I don't mean that he tormented his pupils. He wouldn't have been allowed to get away with it had he tried. These days the balance of power in the classroom has shifted with a vengeance and any tormenting is done by the children. No, as a teacher, he was surprisingly patient and conscientious, a man with real enthusiasm for his subject ('discipline' was the word he preferred to use, being something of an intellectual snob and given to academic jargon) with a surprising talent for communicating that enthusiasm to the children. He was a fairly rigid disciplinarian, but I've never found that children dislike firmness provided a master doesn't indulge in that mordant sarcasm which, by taking advantage of the children's inability to compete, is resented as particularly unfair. He got them through their examinations too. Say what you like, that's something middle-class kids and their parents appreciate. I'm sorry to have slipped into using the word 'kids', that modern shibboleth with its blend of condescension and sycophancy. Vinson never used it. It was his habit to talk about the alumni of the sixth. At first I thought it was an attempt at mildly pompous humour, but now I wonder. He wasn't really a humorous man. The rigid muscles of his face seldom cracked into a smile and when they did it was as disconcerting as a painful grimace. With his lean, slightly stooping figure, the grave eyes behind the horn-rimmed spectacles, the lines etched deeply from the nose to the corners of his unyielding mouth, he looked deceptively what we all thought he was – a middle-aged, disagreeable and not very happy pedant.

No, it wasn't his precious alumni whom he bullied and tyrannised over. It was his wife. The first time I saw Emily Vinson was when I sat next to her at Founder's Memorial Day, an archaic function inherited from the grammar school and regarded with such reverence that even those masters' wives who seldom showed their faces at the school felt obliged to make an appearance.

She was, I guessed, almost twenty years younger than her husband, a thin, anxious-looking woman with auburn hair which had faded early and the very pale, transparent skin which often goes with that colouring. She was expensively and smartly dressed – too incongruously smartly for such a nondescript woman so that the ill-chosen, too-fashionable suit merely emphasised her frail ordinariness. But her eyes were remarkable, an unusual grey-green, huge and slightly exophthalmic under the arched narrow eyebrows. She seldom turned them on me, but when, from time to time, she gave me a swift elliptical glance it was as astounding as turning over an amateurish Victorian oil and discovering a Corot.

It was at the end of Founder's Memorial Day that I received my first invitation to visit them at their home. I found that they lived in some style. She had inherited from her father a small but perfectly proportioned Georgian house which stood alone in some two acres of ground with lawns slanting green down to the river. Apparently her father was a builder who had bought the house cheaply from its impoverished owner with the idea of demolishing it and building a block of flats. The planning authority had slapped on a preservation order just in time and he had died in weeks, no doubt from chagrin, leaving the house and its contents to his daughter. Neither Harold Vinson nor his wife seemed to appreciate their possession. He grumbled about the expense; she grumbled about the housework. The perfectly proportioned façade, so beautiful that it took the breath, seemed to leave them as unmoved as if they lived in a square brick box. Even the furniture, which had been bought with the house, was regarded by them with as little respect as if it were cheap reproduction. When at the end of my first visit I complimented Vinson on the spaciousness and proportions of the dining room he replied:

'A house is only the space between four walls. What does it matter if they are far apart or close together, or what they are made of? You're still in a cage.' His wife was carrying the plates into the kitchen at the time and didn't hear him. He spoke so low that I scarcely heard him myself. I am not even sure now that I was meant to hear.

Marriage is both the most public and the most secret of institutions, its miseries as irritatingly insistent as a hacking cough, its private malaise less easily diagnosed. And nothing is so destructive as unhappiness to social life. No one wants to sit in embarrassed silence while his host and hostess demonstrate their mutual incompatibility and dislike. She could, it seemed, hardly open her mouth without annoying him. No opinion she expressed was worth listening to. Her small domestic chat – which was, after all, all she had – invariably provoked him by its banality so that he would put down his knife and fork with a look of patient resigned boredom as soon as, with a nervous preparatory glance at him, she would steel herself to speak. If she had been an animal, cringing away with that histrionic, essentially false look of piteous entreaty, I can see that the temptation to kick would be irresistible. And, verbally, Vinson kicked.

Not surprisingly they had few friends. Looking back it would probably be more true to say that they had no real friends. The only colleague of his who visited from the school, apart from myself, was Vera Pelling, the junior science teacher, and she, poor girl, was such an unattractive bore that there weren't many alternatives open to her. Vera Pelling is the living refutation of that theory so beloved, I understand, of beauty and fashion journalists in women's magazines that any woman if she takes the trouble can make something of her appearance. Nothing could be done about Vera's pig-like eyes and non-existent chin, and, reasonably enough, she didn't try. I am sorry if I sound harsh. She wasn't a bad sort. And if she thought that making a fourth with me at an occasional free supper with the Vinsons was better than eating alone in her furnished flat I suppose she had her reasons, as I had mine. I never remember having visited the Vinsons without Vera although Emily came to my flat on three occasions, with Harold's approval, to sit for her portrait. It wasn't a success. The result looked like a pastiche of an early Stanley Spencer. Whatever it was I was trying to capture, that sense of a secret life conveyed in the rare grey-green flash of those remarkable eyes, I didn't succeed. When Vinson saw the portrait he said:

'You were prudent, my boy, to opt for teaching as a livelihood. Although, looking at this effort, I would say that the choice was hardly voluntary.' For once I was tempted to agree with him.

Vera Pelling and I became oddly obsessed with the Vinsons. Walking home after one of their supper parties we would mull over the traumas of the evening like an old married couple perennially discussing the inadequacies of a couple of relatives whom we actively disliked but couldn't bear not to see. Vera was a tolerable mimic and would imitate Vinson's desiccated tones.

'My dear, I think that you recounted that not very interesting domestic drama last time we had supper together.'

'And what, my dear, have you been doing with yourself today? What fascinating conversation did you have with the estimable Mrs Wilcox while you cleaned the drawing room together?'

Really, confided Vera, tucking her arm through mine, it had become so embarrassing that it was almost enough to put her off visiting them. But not quite enough apparently. Which was why she, too, was at the Vinsons' on the night when it happened.

On the evening of the crime – the phrase has a stereotyped but dramatic ring which isn't inappropriate to

what, look at it as you will, was no ordinary villainy –
Vera and I were due at the school at 7 p.m. to help with
the dress rehearsal of the school play. I was responsible
for the painted backcloth and some of the props, and Vera
for the make-up. It was an awkward time, too early for
a proper meal beforehand and too late to make it sensible to stay on at school without some thought of supper,
and when Emily Vinson issued through her husband
an invitation to both Vera and me to have coffee and
sandwiches at six o'clock it seemed sensible to accept.
Admittedly, Vinson made it plain that the idea was his
wife's. He seemed mildly surprised that she should wish
to entertain us so briefly – insist on entertaining us was
the expression he used. Vinson himself wasn't involved
with the play. He never grudged spending his private
time to give extra tuition in his own subject but made it a
matter of rigid policy never to become involved in what
he described as extramural divertissements appealing
only to the regressed adolescent. He was, however, a keen
chess player and on Wednesday evenings spent the three
hours from nine until midnight at the local chess club,
of which he was secretary. He was a man of meticulous
habit and any school activity on a Wednesday evening
would, in any case, have had to manage without him.

Every detail, every word spoken at that brief and unre-
markable meal – dry ham sandwiches cut too thick and
synthetic coffee – was recounted by Vera and me at the

Crown Court so that it has always intrigued me that I can no longer visualise the scene. I know exactly what happened, of course. I can recall every word. It's just that I can no longer shut my eyes and see the supper table, the four of us seated there, imprinted in colours on the mind's eye. Vera and I said at the trial that both Vinsons seemed more than usually ill at ease, that Harold, in particular, gave us the impression that he wished we weren't there. But that could have been hindsight.

The vital incident, if you can call it that, happened towards the end of the meal. It was so very ordinary at the time, so crucial in retrospect. Emily Vinson, as if uneasily aware of her duties as hostess and of the unaccountable silence which had fallen on the table, made a palpable effort. Looking up with a nervous glance at her husband she said:

'Two such very nice and polite workmen came this morning—' Vinson touched his lips with his paper serviette then crumpled it convulsively. His voice was unusually sharp as he broke in:

'Emily my dear, do you think you could spare us the details of your domestic routine this evening? I've had a particularly tiring day. And I am trying to concentrate my mind on this evening's game.' And that was all.

The dress rehearsal was over by about nine o'clock, as planned, and I told Vera that I had left a library book at the Vinsons' and was anxious to pick it up on the way home. She made no objection. She gave the impression, poor girl, that she was never particularly anxious to get home. It was only a quarter of an hour's brisk walk to the house and, when we arrived, we saw at once that something was wrong. There were two cars, one with a blue light on the roof, and an ambulance parked unobtrusively but unmistakably at the side of the house. Vera and I glanced briefly at each other then ran to the front door. It was shut. Without ringing we dashed round to the side. The back door, leading to the kitchen quarters, was open. I had an immediate impression that the house was peopled with large men; two of them were in uniform. There was, I remember, a policewoman bending over the prone figure of Emily Vinson. And their cleaning woman, Mrs Wilcox, was there too. I heard Vera explaining to a plain-clothes policeman, obviously the senior man present, that we were friends of the Vinsons, that we had been there to supper only that evening. 'What's happened?' she kept asking. 'What's happened?' Before the police could answer, Mrs Wilcox was spitting it all out, eyes bright with self-important outrage and excitement. I sensed that the police wanted to get rid of her, but she wasn't so easily dislodged. And, after all, she had been first on the scene. She knew it all. I heard it in a series of disjointed sentences:

'Knocked on the head – terrible bruise – marks all

over the parquet flooring where he dragged her – only just coming round now – human fiend – head resting on a cushion in the gas stove – the poor darling – came in just in time at nine twenty – always come to watch colour TV with her on Wednesday night – back door open as usual – found the note on the kitchen table.' The figure writhing on the floor, groaning and crying in a series of harsh grunting moans like an animal in travail, suddenly raised herself and spoke coherently.

'I didn't write it! I didn't write it!'

'You mean Mr Vinson tried to kill her?' Vera was incredulous, head turning from Mrs Wilcox to the watchful, inscrutable faces of the police. The senior officer broke in:

'Now Mrs Wilcox, I think it's time you went home. The ambulance is here. An officer will come along for your statement later this evening. We'll look after Mrs Vinson. There's nothing else for you to do.'

He turned to Vera and me. 'If you two were here earlier this evening, I'd like a word. We're fetching Mr Vinson now from his chess club. But if you two will just wait in the sitting room, please.'

Vera said, 'But if he knocked her unconscious and put her head in the gas oven, then why isn't she dead?'

It was Mrs Wilcox who replied, turning triumphantly as she was led out: 'The conversion, that's why. We're on natural gas from this morning. That North Sea stuff. It isn't poisonous. The two men from the Gas Board came just after nine o'clock.'

They were lifting Emily Vinson onto a stretcher now. Her voice came to us in a desperate wail.

'I tried to tell him. You remember? You heard him? I tried to tell him.'

The suicide note was one of the exhibits at Vinson's trial. A document examiner from the forensic science laboratory testified that it was a forgery, a clever forgery but not Mrs Vinson's writing. He couldn't give an opinion on whether it was the work of the husband, although it was certainly written on a page taken from a writing pad found in the desk in the sitting room. It bore no resemblance to the accused's normal writing. But, in his view, it hadn't been written by Mrs Vinson. He gave a number of technical reasons to support his opinion and the jury listened respectfully. But they weren't surprised. They knew that it hadn't been written by Mrs Vinson. She had stood in the witness box and told them so. And they were perfectly clear in their own minds who had written it.

There was other forensic evidence. Mrs Wilcox's 'marks all over the parquet flooring' were reduced to one long but shallow scrape, just inside the sitting-room door. But it was a significant scrape. It had been made by the heels of Emily Vinson's shoes. Traces of the floor polish which she used were found, not on the soles, but on the sides of the scraped heels and there were minute traces of her shoe polish in the scrape.

The fingerprint officer gave evidence. I hadn't realised until then that fingerprint experts are mostly civilians. It must be a dull job, that constant and meticulous examination of surfaces for the telltale composites and whirls. Hard on the eyes, I should think. In this case, the significance was that he hadn't found any prints. The gas taps had been wiped clean. I could see the jury physically perk up at the news. That was a mistake, all right. It didn't need the prosecution to point out that the taps should have shown Mrs Vinson's prints. She, after all, had cooked their last meal. A cleverer murderer would merely have worn gloves, smudging any existing prints but ensuring that he left none of his own. It had been an over-precaution to wipe the gas taps clean.

Emily Vinson – quiet, distressed but gallant, obviously reluctant to testify against her husband – was remarkably competent in the witness box. I hardly recognised her. No, she hadn't told her husband that she and Mrs Wilcox had arranged to watch the television together shortly after nine o'clock. Mrs Wilcox, who lived nearby, usually did come across to spend a couple of hours with her on Wednesday nights when Mr Vinson was at his chess club. No, she hadn't liked to tell Mr Vinson. Mr Vinson wasn't very fond of inviting people in. The message came over to the jury as clearly as if she had spelt it out – the picture of a downtrodden, unintellectual wife craving the human companionship which her husband denied her, guiltily watching a popular TV show with her cleaning woman at a time when she would be certain that her husband wouldn't catch them out. I glanced at his proud, unyielding mask, at the hands clutched over the edge of the dock, and imagined what he was thinking, what he would have said:

'Surely you have enough of domestic trivia and Mrs Wilcox's conversation – hardly exciting, I should have thought – without inviting her into your drawing room. The woman should know her place.'

The trial didn't take long. Vinson made no defence except to reiterate stubbornly, eyes fixed straight ahead, that he hadn't done it. His counsel did his best, but with the dogged persistence of a man resigned to failure, and the jury had the look of people glad to be faced, for once, with a clear-cut case they could actually understand. The verdict was inevitable. And the subsequent divorce hearing was even shorter. It isn't difficult to persuade a judge that your marriage has irretrievably broken down when your husband is serving a prison sentence for attempted murder.

Two months after the decree absolute we married and I took over the Georgian house, the river view, the Regency furniture. With the physical possessions,

I knew exactly what I was getting. With my wife, I wasn't so sure. There had been something disturbing, even a little frightening, about the competence with which she had carried out my instructions. It hadn't, of course, been particularly difficult. We had planned it together during those sessions when I was painting her portrait. I had written and handed her the fake suicide note on the paper she had supplied a few days before our plans matured. We knew when the gas was due to be converted. She had, as instructed, placed the note on the kitchen table before scraping the heels of her shoes across the polished floor. She had even managed beautifully the only tricky part, to bang the back of her head sufficiently hard against the kitchen wall to raise an impressive bruise but not sufficiently hard to risk bungling the final preparations; the cushion placed in the bottom of the oven for the head, the gas tap turned on and then wiped clean with her handkerchief.

And who could have imagined that she was such a consummate actress? Sometimes, remembering that anguished animal cry of 'I tried to tell him . . . I tried to tell him', I wonder again what is going on behind those extraordinary eyes. She still acts, of course. I find it remarkably irritating, that habit she has particularly when we are in company, of turning on me that meek, supplicating, beaten-dog expression whenever I talk to her. It provokes unkindness. Perhaps it's intended to. I'm afraid I'm beginning to get rather a reputation for sadism. People don't seem to want to come to the house any more.

There is one solution, of course, and I can't pretend that I haven't pondered it. A man who has killed another merely to get his house isn't likely to be too fastidious about killing again. And it was murder; I have to accept that.

Vinson only served nine months of his sentence before dying in the prison hospital of what should have been an uncomplicated attack of influenza. Perhaps his job really was his life, and without his precious alumni the will to live snapped. Or perhaps he didn't choose to live with the memory of his wife's great betrayal. Beneath the petty tyranny, the impatience, the acerbity, there may have been love of a kind.

But the surest option is barred to me. A month ago Emily explained, meekly, like a child propounding a problem, and with a swift sidelong glance, that she had written a confession and left it with her solicitor.

'Just in case anything happens to me, darling.'

She explained that what we did to poor Harold is preying on her mind but that she feels better now that all the details are written down and she can be sure that, after her death, the truth will at last be known and Harold's memory cleared. She couldn't have made it more plain to me that it is in my interest to see that I die first.

I killed Harold Vinson to get the house; Emily, to get me. On the whole, she made the better bargain. In a few weeks I shall lose the house. Emily is selling it. After all, there's nothing I can do to stop her; the place belongs to her not me.

After we married I gave up the teaching post, finding it embarrassing to meet my colleagues as Emily's husband. It was not that anyone suspected. Why should they? I had a perfect alibi for the time of the crime. But I had a dream that, living in that perfection, I might become a painter after all. That was the greatest illusion of all.

So now they are taking down from the end of the drive the board which states 'This Desirable Residence for Sale'. Emily got a very good price for the house and the furniture. More than enough to buy the small but pretentious brick box on an executive estate in North London which will be my cage from now on. Everything is sold. We're taking nothing with us except the gas stove. But, as Emily pointed out when I remonstrated, why not? It's in perfectly good working order.

Mr Millcroft's Birthday

Mildred Millcroft, seated in the front left-hand seat of the Jaguar, thumped her copy of *The Times* into a manageable shape for reading the social pages.

She said, 'I see from the paper that Father shares his birthday with a number of distinguished people.' She read out their names and added, 'That would please him. Quite a coincidence.'

Rodney Millcroft grunted. Since neither their father nor either of them personally knew any of the distinguished people mentioned, he couldn't see why Mildred regarded the felicitously shared birthday as a coincidence. He wished, too, that she wouldn't read the paper while he was driving. The perpetual rustle distracted him and, more dangerously, she was apt to turn over the pages with a flourish of disjointed leaves which momentarily obscured his vision. It was a relief when she completed her scrutiny of the Court pages and the Births, Marriages and Deaths, banged the paper into shape, although hardly the shape the publisher intended, and tossed it on top of the wicker picnic basket on the back seat. She was now able to give her attention to the purpose of their journey.

'I've put in a bottle of Pouilly-Fuissé as well as a Thermos of coffee. If Mrs Doggett puts it in the fridge as soon as we arrive it should be drinkable before we leave.'

Rodney Millcroft's glance was fixed on the road ahead. 'Father has never liked white wine, except for champagne.'

'I daresay not, but I thought champagne was going a bit far. Mrs Doggett would hardly like champagne corks popping all over Meadowsweet Croft. It's upsetting for the other residents.'

Her brother could have pointed out that for a mild, three-person celebration it was only necessary for one cork to pop, and that this was hardly likely to provoke a bacchanalia among the elderly residents of Meadowsweet Croft. He was, however, not disposed to argue. On the subject of their father the two were as one, their alliance, offensive and defensive, against that difficult old man had for over twenty years given an appearance of sibling amity which, without this common and reconciling irritant, it would have been hard for them to sustain. He said, 'This was a particularly awkward day for me to get away. I had to rearrange a number of appointments at considerable inconvenience to important patients.'

Rodney Millcroft was a consultant dermatologist with a large and highly lucrative practice which caused him little trouble. His patients rarely called him out at night, never died on him and, since they were as difficult to cure as they were to kill, he had them for life. Mildred could have pointed out that the day wasn't a particularly convenient one for her either. It had meant missing the Finance and General Purposes Committee of the District Council, who could hardly be expected to arrive at sensible decisions without her. In addition, it was she who had had the trouble of preparing the picnic. Mrs Doggett, the warden of Meadowsweet Croft, had telephoned to say that a tea party for the residents had been arranged for four o'clock complete with birthday cake, and it was to avoid this gruesome celebration that Mildred had said firmly that they could be there for luncheon only and would bring a picnic to be eaten either in their father's room or in the garden. Since she, too, would be sharing it she had taken some trouble. The picnic basket contained salads, smoked salmon, tongue, cold chicken, with fruit salad and cream to follow. Enumerating these delights, she said, 'I only hope he appreciates it.'

'Since he has shown no sign of appreciating either of us for the last forty years he is hardly likely to begin now, even under the stimulus of a bottle of Pouilly-Fuissé and the heady excitement of his eightieth birthday.'

'I suppose he would argue that he passed over to us Uncle Mortimer's three million and that was appreciation enough. He'd probably say that he'd been generous.'

Rodney said, 'That wasn't generosity, merely an extremely sensible and legal device for avoiding Capital Transfer Tax at death. It was family money, anyway. Incidentally, he made the gift seven years ago today. He can die tomorrow and it will all be tax free.'

Both reflected that this was, indeed, a birthday well worth celebrating. But Mildred reverted to a perennial grievance.

'He has no intention of dying, and I don't blame him. He can live another twenty years for all I care. I only wish he'd drop this obsession about moving to Maitland Lodge. He's perfectly well looked after at Meadowsweet Croft. The home is extremely well run and Mrs Doggett is a most capable and experienced woman. The local authority have a very good reputation for their geriatric services. He's lucky to be there.'

Her brother changed gear and turned carefully into the suburban road leading to the home.

'Well, if he thinks we're going to find over sixty thousand a year between us to pay for a place at Maitland Lodge, it's time he faced reality. The idea is ludicrous.'

They had had this conversation many times before. Mildred said, 'It's only because that dreadful old Brigadier is there and keeps visiting Father and telling him how wonderful the place is. I think he even took Father to spend a day there. And it's not even as if they're old friends. Father only met him on the golf course. The

Brigadier is a bad influence on Father in every way. I don't know why they let him out of Maitland Lodge. He seems to be able to hire cars and travel the whole country at will. If he's so old and frail that he needs to be in a Home they should see that he stays there.'

Both Rodney and Mildred had every intention of seeing that their father, Augustus, stayed in Meadowsweet Croft. Although eighty, he was not particularly frail, but a total inability to cook for himself or, indeed, do anything which he regarded as women's work, coupled with an acerbic tongue which had driven away a succession of housekeepers except those who had been alcoholic, mad or kleptomaniac had made residential care inevitable. It had taken his children considerable time and trouble to persuade him into Meadowsweet Croft. The relief for them, if not for him, had been considerable. They told him on their infrequent visits that he was a very fortunate old man. He even had a room to himself where he was able to display the results of his lifelong hobby, a collection of ships in bottles.

Meadowsweet Croft was nowhere near a meadow, nor was it a croft and it could only have been described as 'sweet' by a visitor partial to the smell of lemon-scented furniture polish. It was, however, very well run, almost aggressively clean and the diet so carefully balanced in accordance with modern theories about the feeding of the elderly that it would have been perverse to expect it also to be palatable. Mrs Doggett was a State Registered Nurse but preferred not to use the title or wear her uniform since, after all, Meadowsweet Croft was not meant to be a nursing home and her old dears shouldn't be encouraged to think of themselves as invalids. She encouraged exercise, positive thinking and meaningful activity and was occasionally a little discouraged to realise that all the activity her residents wanted was to watch television in the lounge with their chair backs placed firmly against the wall as if to guard against the possibility of anyone creeping up on them during the more enthralling moments of *Midsomer Murders* or *Wallander*. They had had a lifetime of exercise, positive thinking and meaningful activity. It has to be said that Mrs Doggett and the residents in general got on very well together, with the exception of one central misunderstanding; she took the view that the old people hadn't come to Meadowsweet Croft in order to live a life of self-indulgent idleness, and the old people thought that they had. But they recognised that there were worse places than this – the grave for one – and when Mrs Doggett proclaimed, as she frequently did, that she loved her old dears, really loved them, she spoke no more than the truth. In order to love them the more effectively she made sure that they were never out of her sight.

This constant surveillance was helped by the

architecture of the home. It was a single-storey, U-shaped building built round a courtyard with a central lawn, a single tree which obstinately refused to thrive, and four precisely arranged flowerbeds which were planted with bulbs in the spring, geraniums in the summer and dahlias in the autumn. The courtyard was furnished with solid wooden benches so that the residents could, in summer, take the sun. Each bore a plaque with the name of the person it commemorated, a memento mori which might have distressed users less tough than Mrs Doggett's old dears. The benches, not built for comfort, were solidly constructed and practically indestructible, and their occupants had no intention of adding to them.

It isn't easy to manage a satisfactory picnic sitting in line on a hard bench with no table. Mildred had thoughtfully provided large paper napkins, and they sat in a row with these on their laps while she passed plates of salmon and ham and distributed lettuce leaves and tomatoes. The other benches were unoccupied – the residents had no great love of fresh air – but the picnickers were watched by interested eyes while, across the courtyard, Mrs Doggett occasionally waved an encouraging hand from her office window. Augustus Millcroft ate heartily but in silence. Conversation was perfunctory until the fruit salad was finished when, as his children expected, he embarked on his old grievance.

They listened in silence, then Rodney Millcroft said,

'I'm sorry Father, but the idea is impossible. Maitland Lodge costs sixty thousand a year and the fees will almost certainly rise. It would be an insupportable drain on our capital.'

'The capital which you wouldn't have had if it weren't for me.'

'You passed over to Mildred and me the greater part of Uncle Mortimer's legacy and naturally we're grateful. We can assure you that the money hasn't been wasted. You wouldn't have made over the capital if you hadn't had confidence in our financial probity and acumen.'

'I didn't see why the bloody government should get it.'

'Precisely.'

'But now I don't see why I shouldn't have a bit of comfort in my old age.'

'Father, you're perfectly comfortable here. This garden really is delightful.'

'This garden is Hell.'

Rodney said, 'In leaving the capital to you, I'm sure Uncle Mortimer thought of it as family money to be properly invested and left in turn to your children and grandchildren.'

'Mortimer never intended anything of the sort. That last Christmas, when we were all together at Pentlands, the Christmas he died, he told me that he was proposing to send for his solicitor as soon as the office opened after the holiday, and to change his will.'

Rodney said, 'A passing fancy. Old people get them. It's as well that he never got the chance.'

His father said, 'No. I saw to that. That's why I murdered him.'

Mildred felt that the only possible response to this statement was, 'What on earth are you saying, Father?' It was, however, a question which it was hardly logical to ask. Her father's voice had been embarrassingly loud and clear. While she was searching for a reasonable response, her brother said calmly, 'That's absolutely ridiculous, Father. Murdered him? How did you murder him?'

'With arsenic.'

Mildred had found her voice. She said, 'Uncle Mortimer died of a bad heart and viral pneumonia complicated by gastroenteritis.'

'Complicated by arsenic.'

'Where did you get arsenic, Father?' Rodney's voice was studiously calm. Unlike his sister who was perched rigidly upright on the edge of her seat, he stretched back in as relaxed a pose as the hardness of the bench permitted, like a man who is prepared to waste a little time indulging his father's senile fantasy.

'I got it from Smallbone, your uncle's gardener. He used to say there was nothing like arsenic for dealing with dandelions. When Mortimer found out he pronounced that the stuff was too dangerous to have about the place and made Smallbone destroy it. But Smallbone kept a small quantity of the arsenic for himself in one of those old-fashioned blue poison bottles. He told me that having it gave him a feeling of power. I can understand that. Knowing his opinion of his employer, I'm only surprised that he didn't use it on Mortimer before I did. I knew where he'd hidden it in the garden shed, so when he died I hid it even more securely. It gave me a sense of power, too. Smallbone always said that arsenic didn't deteriorate with age, and he was certainly right there.'

Rodney said sarcastically, 'And I suppose you administered it to Uncle in his medicine and, despite its well-known appalling taste, he drank it down immediately.'

His father didn't at once reply. His sideway glance at his children was one of reluctant cunning mixed with a certain self-satisfaction. He said, 'I suppose I'd better tell you the whole of it now that I've begun.'

Rodney said repressively, 'You certainly had. It's a complete fabrication, of course, but we may as well hear the whole story now that you've embarked on it.'

'You remember that one-pound box of soft-centred Belgian chocolates that you brought your uncle for Christmas? I may as well say that he regarded it as a deplorably inadequate present. That may have been one of the reasons which led to his decision to change the will.'

Mildred said, 'Uncle Mortimer was addicted to soft-centred chocolates, and they were the most expensive we could buy.'

'Oh I know that. You both spoke about the cost so frequently and so openly that I've no doubt his nurse, Mrs Jennings – who is still alive, incidentally – will remember the gift. The arsenic I had was in the form of a white powder. I removed the base of the peppermint chocolate with a small, sharp knife and replaced the peppermint cream with arsenic. I can't pretend the method was original but it was certainly effective.'

His son said, 'A fiddling job, surely. It can't have been easy without fear of subsequent detection.'

'It was a comparatively simple task for someone who has succeeded in building the *Cutty Sark* in a gin bottle. But your uncle wasn't after all going to examine the chocolate closely. I propped him up in bed and popped it into his mouth. He took one bite and swallowed it.'

'Without complaining about the taste?'

'Oh he complained about the taste, but I immediately popped in a raspberry cream and washed it down with a stiff dose of gin. He wasn't entirely compos mentis at the time. It was easy to convince him that he'd been mistaken about the bitterness of the first bite.'

'And what did you do with the bottle of arsenic?'

There was a second pause, a second look of sly cunning. Then their father said, 'I hid it in the blasted oak.'

No explanation was necessary. Both his children knew precisely what he meant. The large oak tree on the outskirts of the grounds of Pentlands had been their tree in childhood, as it had been their father's. It had been struck by lightning in a notable storm in the early 1900s but still stood, the boughs providing a wonderful climbing frame, its split trunk a hiding place large enough to conceal a small child.

Rodney Millcroft said, 'All this is, of course, a fantasy, but I advise you to say nothing about it to anyone else. It may be amusing to you, and no doubt you take pleasure in its ingenuity, but other people may take a different view.'

Mildred had been thinking. Suddenly she said, 'I don't believe Uncle Mortimer seriously intended for a moment to alter his will. Why should he?'

'He disliked the thought of his money eventually coming to either of you. You, Rodney, had particularly displeased him. You insulted the woman to whom he was deeply, indeed passionately, devoted.'

'What woman? I never even knew Aunt Maud.'

'Not Aunt Maud – Mrs Thatcher. You said you would rather dive into a tank of piranha fish than be a member of her Cabinet.'

'It was spoken in jest.'

'A jest in very poor taste. Your perverted sense of humour could have lost our side of the family a considerable fortune if I hadn't remembered the arsenic.'

Mildred said, 'But what about me? What am I supposed to have done?'

'With you it was more a question of being rather than doing. Greedy, selfish, tactless and self-opinionated were some of the words he used. He said that God had given you a moustache to mark his regret at having made you a woman. Other remarks, which I'll spare you, were frankly uncomplimentary.'

Mildred was surprisingly unperturbed by this diatribe. She said, 'That proves it. Obviously he was deranged. But if Uncle Mortimer meant to change his will, did he tell you to whom he proposed to leave the money? He had a great family sense for all his faults. I really can't see him leaving it out of the family.'

'Oh he proposed to leave it in the family, all right. It was all to go to the Australian cousins.'

Mildred was outraged. 'But he hadn't seen them for forty years! And they didn't need it. They've got millions of sheep.'

'Perhaps he thought they could do with a few million more.'

Rodney's voice was quietly ominous. 'Why are you telling us all this, Father?'

'Because my conscience is troubling me. I'm an old man now, coming to the end of my earthly journey. I feel I need to confess, to make my peace with the world and my Maker. You two have been for seven years in possession of money to which neither of you has any right. I had no right to inherit the three million in the first place and certainly no right to pass it on. These things weigh on an old man's mind. The air, indeed the whole atmosphere of Meadowsweet Croft is conducive, I find, to feelings of guilt and remorse. Take the Sunday visits of the Reverend Hinkley when he and the members of his Women's Bright Hour sing hymns for us round the piano in the lounge. Then Mrs Doggett insists on turning on Radio Four very loudly every morning for 'Thought for the Day'. And of course, we have the children from the local comprehensive school who come to sing carols for us at Christmas, and the local church magazine brought round to us every month by the vicar's wife, always with a little encouraging homily. All these things have their effect. And then there's the food here, the unutterable boredom of the other residents, Mrs Doggett's voice and incipient halitosis, and the hardness of the beds; constant if petty reminders of that Hell which is supposed to await the unrepentant sinner. Not that I totally believe in eternal punishment, of course, but being required to live at Meadowsweet Croft does dispose one to a certain morbidity of mind.'

There was a long silence. Then Rodney said, 'This, of course, is blackmail, and blackmail of a particularly inept kind. No one will believe you. The story will be taken as the ravings of an old man well advanced in senility.'

'Ah, but they can see I'm not, can't they?'

Rodney went on. 'And who do you expect to believe you?'

'The Australian cousins may well. I feel particularly guilty about your Australian cousins. But it won't matter whether they do or not. There will certainly be in everyone's mind a very large element of doubt. As I said, it was a pity you made such a big thing of buying your uncle those chocolates. And then there's the fact that I passed the money over to you. That might look very like blackmail. I must say I don't think the District Council will like the story, Mildred. And as far as you're concerned, Rodney, I've a feeling that your most lucrative patients will be taking their acne elsewhere.'

The silence this time was both long and profound. Then Rodney said, 'We'll think it over. We'll let you know our decision the day after tomorrow. In the meantime, do or say nothing. Do you understand me, Father? Nothing.'

The conversation had been so upsetting to Rodney and Mildred that they left Meadowsweet Croft without retrieving the Pouilly-Fuissé from the refrigerator. Mrs Doggett felt justified in confiscating it as a raffle prize at the summer fund-raising fête of the League of Friends. So Mr Millcroft never got his celebration drink, but he was consoled in his disappointment less by his aversion to white wine than by the knowledge that his children's birthday visit had really gone better than he could have hoped.

As soon as they had thrown off the suburbs of the town and were on a quiet country road, Rodney drove the car onto the verge and turned off the engine. There were decisions to be made to which both of them felt they could hardly give adequate thought in a moving vehicle. After a few minutes Mildred said, 'The whole thing is ridiculous, of course. The brothers never liked each other, but I don't think Father would go as far as murder. Still, it's just as well that Uncle was cremated. The doctor, apparently, never had the least suspicion.'

'Doctors who make a practice of suspecting their middle-class acquaintances of murdering their relatives usually end up without any patients. Uncle Mortimer was dying, in any case. If Father did murder him' – Rodney had some difficulty in getting out the word – 'a confession can't bring him back.'

Brother and sister took some comfort from the undeniable fact that nothing could bring Uncle back. Then Mildred spoke what was in both their minds.

'It would only be a couple of miles out of our way to go to Pentlands. If Father did throw the bottle into the oak it's probably still there. Without the evidence no one will take his story seriously. There's no point in putting it off. Now is as good a time as any.'

Rodney said, 'Who was it who bought Pentlands? Do you remember? I only know that the executors sold it below its worth.'

'I think they were called Swingleton, an elderly couple without children. They're hardly likely to go climbing oak trees.'

'I doubt that we'll find it easy now. I'm certainly too large to get into the trunk. If the bottle is there we'll have to hook it up.'

'How are we going to do that?'

'I've got my walking stick in the boot of the car.'

Mildred said, 'Of course we may have trouble in actually finding it. Even on a bright May day like this it will be very dark inside the trunk.'

Rodney spoke with some satisfaction. 'I never drive without a torch. We can use that. The problem may be getting into the grounds. If the gate is locked we'll have to get over the wall. Well, we've done that often enough in our time.'

Unfortunately the gate was locked. Although the stone wall was not more than five feet high, they had considerable difficulty in getting over and only managed it in the end with the help of a folding picnic chair from the back of the car. There was also the problem of passing motorists. Twice they had to desist at the sound of an approaching car, pick up the chair and peer in the grass verge as if searching for rare plants. Rodney in particular found it difficult to hoist up his sister while keeping his eyes and ears open, and Mildred's tight skirt was an embarrassing hindrance. There is something peculiarly unedifying about the sight of a stout lady of forty-five stuck on the top of a wall with her legs waving, her skirt ruffled up to expose an undignified expanse of white knickers. He trembled to think what Sir Fortescue Lackland, his most distinguished patient, would think if he could see them now, and was only fortified to continue with the expedition by the thought of what Sir Fortescue would think if Father ever carried out his threat and confessed.

Eventually, however, they were over and, folding up the chair and picking up the walking stick, crept along the inner side of the wall towards the blasted oak. With the help of the chair Rodney had no problem in reaching the necessary height and in peering down into the dark depths of the trunk. Mildred handed up the torch and he shone it down, illuminating the bed of shrivelled leaves, dried acorns, small twigs, broken pieces of bark and a twisted white plastic bag. And beside the bag he could see something a great deal more interesting: a small dark blue bottle with ridged sides.

Mildred called out quietly, 'Is it there? Is it there?'

'Yes, it's here.'

But discovering the bottle was a great deal easier than retrieving it. Rodney found it impossible to manoeuvre the walking stick and at the same time hold the heavy torch, so both of them had to mount the chair, which creaked under their weight and, indeed, seemed in danger of collapsing. That catastrophe was averted when Mildred hooked her left arm round one of the lower boughs, thus releasing some of the weight. She shone the torch steadily into the trunk of the oak while her brother reached down with the stick. His plan was gently to edge the bottle to the side of the trunk, then hook it up. At first, to their horror, they were in danger of losing sight of it when it sank among the soft detritus of dried leaves. At the second try it became entangled with the white plastic bag. But at last Rodney managed to nudge it towards the edge and began the slow, careful, upward lift. Twice it got within reach of his left hand but twice it fell. But on the third attempt, not daring to speak in case even their breath dislodged it, the bottle came within reach of his stretched fingers and he was able to grasp it. Then, with relief, he jumped down from the chair and gave a hand to his sister.

'And what do you think you're doing?'

The voice, which caused them both to jump like startled cats and set their hearts pounding, was calm, authoritative, dismayingly upper class. They turned round and saw two young men in tweed caps and jackets. Mildred's first thought was that they were gamekeepers, but almost immediately she rejected this idea. The grounds of Pentlands were extensive, amounting to two or three acres, but hardly suitable for the rearing of game and the young men looked and spoke more like sons of the house than servants. One of them was actually carrying a gun. It was a moment of complete horror.

Her brother had been rendered speechless with shock and embarrassment but Mildred recovered herself with admirable speed. With an attempt at charm she said, 'I'm afraid you've caught us trespassing. We would have called at the front door and asked permission, but the gate was locked. My brother and I merely wanted to visit our uncle's old family home. We used to play here frequently as children during the holidays and this old tree is a part of our childhood memories. We were driving past and couldn't resist the temptation to visit it.'

The taller young man said coolly, 'Equipped with walking stick and chair. What precisely were you looking for?'

He shot out his hand and took the bottle. Rodney said, 'We saw it lying there and were a little curious. It's nothing to do with us, of course.'

'In that case we'd better take charge of it. It looks like poison to me. We'll see it's safely locked up.' He turned to his companion. 'Henry, do you think it's necessary to phone the police?'

Henry was nonchalant. 'Oh I don't think so. They look comparatively harmless. Almost respectable, indeed, although, of course, you can't tell from appearances. But we'd certainly better take charge of the bottle. And we'll take their names and addresses.'

Rodney said promptly: 'John Smith and Mary Smith. High Street, Tooting Bec.'

The younger man smiled grimly. 'Your real names and addresses, I think. Perhaps you have your driving licence on you. We need some means of identification.'

The procedure of name-taking took place in an embarrassed silence. Afterwards the Millcrofts were escorted to the gate which was locked after them. Dishevelled, dirty and scarlet with shame, they looked like a modern Adam and Eve summarily ejected from Paradise. Neither spoke until they were again seated in the car and Rodney had turned on the engine. Then Mildred said, 'If Father confesses now and it gets into the papers, those two men are bound to come forward. And they've got the evidence.'

Rodney wished that his sister was less liable to state the obvious. Since there was nothing helpful to be said, he said nothing. He was only grateful that Mildred was apparently too dispirited to assail him for his folly in giving a false name. After a short pause, Mildred spoke again.

'Shall you get in touch with Maitland Lodge or shall I?'

In a well-regulated and moral universe, Mr Millcroft would no doubt have found Maitland Lodge a sad disappointment – the food indigestible, the wine undrinkable, the staff draconian, his fellow residents uncongenial and the Brigadier a far less agreeable companion under the same roof than he was as an occasional visitor to Meadowsweet Croft. Regrettably for the triumph of virtue over wickedness, Maitland Lodge more than lived up to Mr Millcroft's hopes and expectations. He and the Brigadier agreed that they could certainly aim to live there for the next ten years before wondering whether it was time to shuffle off this mortal coil. Mr Millcroft was a great favourite with the staff, who regarded him as a 'real character', particularly when he was at his most acerbic. He was especially matey with the buxom Nurse Bunting who occasionally ministered to the residents' aches and pains. When wearing her impeccably starched blue and white uniform and goffered cap Nurse Bunting was a model of professional rectitude. After duty hours, however, she would literally let down her hair and she and Mr Millcroft enjoyed many cosy sessions in his room over his nightcap of hot whisky.

'You are awful about your family, Gussie,' she occasionally protested. 'No visits allowed, no letters, not even a box of chocolates.'

'Particularly not a box of chocolates,' said Mr Millcroft.

One evening in late August, three months after his admission and at the end of a perfect summer day, he and the Brigadier were sitting in their comfortable cushioned wicker chairs on the terrace looking out over the beautiful gardens of Maitland Lodge to the distant shimmer of the river. Badge the butler had just brought out their pre-dinner drinks and both were at peace with the world. The talk reverted, as it often did, to the circumstances under which this happy resolution had been achieved. The Brigadier said, 'I'm still surprised that your children actually swallowed your story.'

'I'm not. People are always ready to believe that others will act as they might have acted themselves. I had no doubt, too, they would call at Pentlands. What was more natural? Your men must have been very convincing, though. Put the fear of God into them. Wish I'd been there to see it.'

'Well,' said the Brigadier easily, 'that's the advantage of being a soldier, you know. You can always find a couple of good chaps when you want a job done.'

'What was it they put in the bottle?'

'You know what it was. Bicarbonate of soda.'

There was a silence while the Brigadier sipped his gin and tonic and Mr Millcroft savoured his dry sherry. It was served at precisely the temperature he liked.

He was pondering whether to try one of the delectable nuts or canapés on the drinks tray or whether that would spoil his appetite for dinner, when the Brigadier said, 'Question I've always wanted to ask you. Not sure whether I should. Some questions shouldn't be asked among friends. Still, a natural curiosity, don't you know. I just wondered – don't answer if you don't want to – whether you did help your brother on his way.'

'Whether I murdered him?'

'Not to put too fine a point on it, yes. Not with arsenic, of course. Only a cad would use arsenic. That's the weapon of suburban poisoners and Victorian adulteresses. Still, there are other ways presumably.'

Mr Millcroft appeared to consider the matter. 'Well, if I had done it, I'd have used something quite simple. A plastic bag, for example. You just slip it over the head when the victim is sleeping, press it down firmly over the nose and mouth and he goes out as gently as a sleeping child. I don't see how anybody could detect that.'

The Brigadier said, 'You'd have to dispose of the bag, though. What would you do about it?'

'Oh,' said Mr Millcroft, taking a further sip of his sherry, 'I'd just throw it into the trunk of the blasted oak.' Then, glancing at his friend's face, he said, 'Just a joke, old man. Just a joke. Pass over the paper, will you. What was it you fancied for tomorrow's two thirty?'

Also by P. D. James

ff

The Mistletoe Murder and Other Stories

As the acknowledged Queen of Crime, P. D. James was frequently commissioned by newspapers and magazines to write a short story for Christmas, and four of the best have been drawn from the archives and published here together for the first time. From the title story about a strained country-house Christmas party, to another about an illicit affair that ends in murder, plus two cases for detective Adam Dalgliesh, these are masterfully atmospheric stories, with the lure of a mystery to be solved.

'A box of crackers.' *Guardian* Books of the Year

'What a pleasure to encounter P. D. James again at the top of her form.' Shirley Hughes

'There are very few writers who can compete with P. D. James at her best.' *Spectator*

ff

An Unsuitable Job for a Woman

Meet Cordelia Gray: twenty-two years-old, tough, intelligent and now sole inheritor of the Pryde Detective Agency. Her first assignment finds her hired by Sir Ronald Callender to investigate the death of his son Mark, a young Cambridge student found hanged in mysterious circumstances. Required to delve into the hidden secrets of the Callender family, Cordelia soon realises it is not a case of suicide, and that the truth is entirely more sinister.

'P. D. James is an addictive writer, [with] a quality of intelligence, a genuine curiosity about character, and an ability to describe the density of little-known lives.'
Anita Brookner

'One of the most compulsive and acutely observed thrillers of the year . . . a study of the complex motives that make up the cold mind of a killer.' *Daily Express*

'A top-rated puzzle of peril that holds you all the way.'
New York Times

ff

The Skull beneath the Skin

Hired to protect a beautiful but neurotic actress, Cordelia Gray soon becomes embroiled in a case as dangerous to her own life as it is mysterious. Clarissa Lisle hopes to make a spectacular comeback in a production of *The Duchess of Malfi*, to be performed in Ambrose Gorringe's sinister castle at Courcy Island. Cordelia is there to ensure her safety following the appearance of a number of poison-pen letters. But it soon becomes clear that all are in danger. Trapped within the walls of the Gothic castle, the treacherous past of the island re-emerges, and everyone seems to have a motive for sending Clarissa 'down, down to hell'.

'A masterly version of the clue-and-alibi game . . . Five-star entertainment.' *Guardian*

'A fine novel . . . From its very first pages you feel you are in marvellously sure hands.' *The Times*

ff

The Children of Men

The year is 2021. No child has been born for twenty-five years. The human race faces extinction. Under the despotic rule of Xan Lyppiatt, the Warden of England, the old are despairing and the young cruel. Theo Faren, a cousin of the Warden, lives a solitary life in this ominous atmosphere. That is, until a chance encounter with a young woman leads him into contact with a group of dissenters. Suddenly his life is changed irrevocably as he faces agonising choices which could affect the future of mankind.

'Taut, terrifying and convincing.' *Daily Mail*

'Extraordinary . . . P. D. James stretches her considerable talents in this daring novel.' *New York Times*

'Spare and disturbing.' *Independent*

ff

Cover Her Face

St Cedd's Church fête has been held in the grounds of Martingale manor house for generations. As if organising stalls, as well as presiding over luncheon, the bishop and the tea tent, were not enough for Mrs Maxie on that mellow July afternoon, she also has to contend with the news of her son's sudden engagement to her new parlour maid, Sally Jupp. On the following morning Martingale and the village are shocked by the discover of Sally's body. Investigating the violent death at the manor house, Detective Chief Inspector Adam Dalgliesh is embroiled in the complicated passions beneath the calm surface of English village life.

'A classic story of English rural murder.' *The Times*

'There are very few thriller writers who can compete with P. D. James at her best.' *Spectator*